CAPTAIN MORETTI'S
DAUGHTER

By Sally E. DiPaula

Nicholson
Books

CAPTAIN MORETTI'S DAUGHTER

Printed in the United States of America

10 9 8 7 6 5 4 3 2 1

ISBN-13: 978-1-963102-64-2 (Paperback)
ISBN-13: 978-1-963102-63-5 (eBook)
ISBN-13: 978-1-963102-65-9 (Hardcover)

Nicholson
Books

To Charlotte

CHAPTER 1

The Dodger

A man—his stink strong even from the doorway the Dodger is hiding in—hobbles up and stops in front of the tavern's garbage can. The Dodger could walk past him to the alley's entrance. The man looks so drunk, he probably wouldn't be able to describe the Dodger to the police, and they probably wouldn't take the description seriously, anyway. But the Dodger can't take that chance, so he remains in the shadows.

The drunk lifts the lid off the trash can and pokes his head and right hand in it at the same time. The smell doesn't seem to bother him—most likely, it's no worse than the smell coming off his own body. He extends his hand further into the can and stops. Did he find some food, or did he find what the Dodger just dumped in there? Whichever it is, he tugs at it hard.

His face is buried deep within the metal can when he stops tugging, jerks his head out, and vomits. He's found the body. What will he do now? Knock on the back door of the tavern? Call the police? No, he's just an old drunk. He stumbles out of the alley. Once he's out of sight, the Dodger follows. Time for him to get back to the ship. But first, he needs to meet with someone. It's a meeting he's not looking forward to.

CHAPTER 2

Frankie

I'm lurking in the hall, or "foy-yay," as Aunt Bess calls it. I'm not supposed to be. I'm supposed to be in my room in the attic. But I need to know what they are saying. My future depends on it. And as far as I'm concerned, my *life* depends on it.

Very carefully, I peek into the living room. I see my father sitting next to the new RCA TV, hands on his knees, and looking like he's ready to jump up and run. Aunt Bess is sitting across from him, doing all the talking.

"It can't go on like this, Flavio. I just can't handle her. She never listens to a thing I say, and I never know what she's going to do next. Frances is so disruptive that even our boys have complained."

That's a laugh. Her boys are the ones always starting the trouble, and I'm the one always getting the blame. And I've told my aunt a million times that my name isn't Frances. My friends call me Frankie, but my real name is Francesca, Francesca Moretti, which is an Italian name that my aunt never uses because she doesn't approve of Italians.

"Your boarding school idea didn't work, obviously. How she managed to get thrown out of two in as many months is beyond me. We'll never be able to find another boarding school to take her now. Her behavior the last few months is more than anyone can take. I don't know how to resolve this. I really don't." She opens her eyes so wide that her arching eyebrows are hidden by her stubby bangs. That look means it is, finally, my father's turn to speak. Not knowing her as well as I do, he doesn't get the signal.

He's sitting on the kind of sofa you'd expect in this house with all that gold, swirly material that sticks out. My aunt and uncle are sitting in easy chairs that match the sofa. "Brocade," she calls it. These are the chairs they sit in every night while I sit on the sofa with my cousins, Ronald and Gerald. Aunt Bess knits things (her latest is an orange and blue scarf for me); Uncle Ronnie reads three newspapers; and my cousins and I read the books they assign us. We aren't allowed to watch much TV because my aunt read in a magazine that the rays coming off televisions are bad for our health. Before I moved in with her and Uncle Ronnie, I watched TV every night with my Mom, and my health is just fine.

"Well?" Aunt Bess finally says when my father doesn't respond to her wide-eyed signal.

He stands up and looks down at my aunt and uncle, then yells, "Francesca!"

I'm there in two seconds.

"Francesca, go pack some clothes, warm clothes. It will be cold on the ship."

He's taking me with him!

I run to my bedroom in the attic and pull my suitcase from under the bed. I've been packing and repacking it, ready to go since the day he left after Mom's funeral five months ago. I prayed and prayed he'd come back for me some day. Now, he has.

I make sure I have plenty of warm clothes, along with my textbooks, my passport, Kotex and Clearasil. I pick up the orange and blue scarf my aunt knitted for me, then decide to leave it.

In the taxi on the way to my father's ship, he looks at me oddly.

"What happened to your hair, Francesca?" A good question since it used to be long enough to put in a ponytail.

"Aunt Bess made me get it cut right before I went to the first boarding school. She said it was too unruly." My father runs his hand over my scalp and makes an *oomph* kind of sound.

"Do you like it short?" he asks me.

"No, I hate it. I want to let it grow."

He nods and smiles.

He doesn't say much else on the way to *Il Destino*. It's an Italian Merchant Marine freighter that sails all over the world, and he's the captain.

"I don't know how long this will work, Francesca, you living on the ship. There's your schooling—" I start to interrupt, but he keeps talking. "And I don't know what they will say when they find out."

"Who's 'they,' Papa?"

"My bosses, *Cara Mia*. The Home Office. A ship is no place for a girl, Francesca, especially a teen-aged girl. You know that. We talked about it when your mother died."

We reach the port. I've been here before, almost every time Papa visited Mom and me. It hasn't changed; lots of people—seamen and longshoremen and government men—running around and between trucks and cars and trolleys and cranes. And the smell is the same as always—like a gas station with a leaky pump that's next door to a septic tank that also has a leak.

The taxi rumbles over railroad tracks and weaves through the people and machines. As we reach his ship, my father sits forward in his seat and stares out the windshield. I sit forward, too, and that's when I see what he's looking at.

Two police cars parked at the bottom of the gangway.

CHAPTER 3

The Dodger

The room he's in is claustrophobic, with its peeling wallpaper and odor of rancid cooking oil. The holes in the plaster on the wall behind the desk reveal reddish brown bricks, the cement holding them together slopped on. Through the closed door comes the sound of ricocheting pool balls and men's rowdy voices. Seated at the desk is a squat, pudgy man in a black silk shirt buttoned tightly around his throat. The man is his boss, the man the Dodger has just told that he failed in his mission.

The boss doesn't look angry, just curious. "What did he do on the ship?"

"He was the Wiper," the Dodger says.

"And what exactly does a Wiper do?

"Cleans the engine, the machines, wipes them down. Menial work."

"Ah," the boss nods and looks satisfied. Then his look changes. "You idiot."

The Dodger has heard him call a lot of people "idiot." He uses it any time he's unhappy with someone.

The Dodger clenches his fists which are held behind his back by the boss's bodyguard.

"You weren't supposed to kill him, not until he told you where it is." With that, the boss nods to the bodyguard. A quick swipe from him sends the Dodger tumbling, but the bodyguard grabs his shirt to keep him from falling to the floor.

"He didn't have it on him. When he said it was hidden and someone would find it eventually, I hit him again. The chair fell backwards, and his head struck the floor. It was an accident."

"You have a lot of accidents, don't you?" the bodyguard whispers in the Dodger's ear. "Like the Leader's secretary. You were supposed to find out who had him plant the bug in the Leader's office, but you never did find out, did you? Because your interrogation got a little too rough, and the secretary was never able to tell us who put him up to it."

The Dodger knows not to give an excuse for that one. The traitorous secretary surprised him by holding out longer than he thought he would, and the Dodger got a little impatient. But that wasn't the case with the Wiper. That really was an accident. The Dodger would have gotten the information out of him eventually. He always did when he assisted the Obersturmbannführer in France during the war.

"So, how do you propose to find it now?"

"It has to be on the ship, right? So, when I'm back on board, I'll search for it."

"Ah, an excellent idea." His smile is not reassuring; nor is his slow, quiet voice. The soft tone disappears. "You root around and see what you can find. Nobody will notice you wandering around the ship when you're supposed to be working. You idiot!"

"I won't always be on duty. I get time off. I'll find it then. You'll see."

"I'd better see. That innocent-looking baby face of yours may have helped you dodge the partisans during the war and the reprisals after-wards, and dodge the consequences of the secretary's death. But if you don't recover the document, if our Leader and our new society is threat-ened because of your incompetence, your dodging will be over. For good."

CHAPTER 4

Frankie

My father is in his cabin with those policemen, and I'm leaning against the rail trying to keep out of the way of all the seamen running back and forth behind me. A few are in uniforms like my father's, but most are in blue jeans and heavy black sweaters. They're not wearing jackets. I guess they're too busy to feel the cold, but I feel it. I'm wearing my camel hair car coat and my gloves and wool cap, and it's so windy, I almost wish I had the scarf Aunt Bess knitted for me.

The men and the cranes are unloading cargo from *Il Destino*—tires, big boxes of typewriters, herbs, and spices for McCormick's, even Alfa Romeos, which my father says are really popular in Italy but not here. He told me that once the longshoremen are finished unloading, they'll load the cargo that *Il Destino* will be carrying to New Orleans and then to Italy.

Il Destino will be carrying me, too. I'm going to live with my Papa all the time now, not just two months a year. So he doesn't worry about my schooling, I'll study every day, and if I have any questions, he can answer them because he's very smart.

Mom always told me that. "You get your brains from your father," she would say every time I brought my report card home. I almost always got all As except in Conduct. But I've never considered that a real subject, so it didn't bother me.

The two policemen are on deck and walking toward the gangway now. Their shoulders are hunched up against the wind, and their eyes are squinting into the bright sun. They're talking to each other so seriously that they don't notice me. Probably think I'm one of the sailors because my ski cap is hiding my chopped-up hair. I walk behind them to see if I can catch what they're saying.

"Why did you tell the captain that the ship could leave tonight, Lieutenant? There's a very good chance the guy who killed the sailor is a member of his crew."

"There is," the lieutenant agrees, "but whether he is or not, our chances of finding him are almost zero. But if we keep the ship in port, I'll tell you what there is a good chance of."

"What's that?" The other policeman stops, and I almost run into him. He doesn't notice because he's looking at the lieutenant.

"There's a good chance that the Longshoremen's Union will complain to the mayor that their men are losing work time money, and the company that owns *Il Destino* will also complain to the mayor that every day the ship sits in port is costing them money. Then the mayor will complain to the commissioner, who will complain to the chief, who will complain to the precinct captain, who will complain to me. Then, I will turn around and tell you to find the killer, which you won't be able to do because we have no evidence, no leads, nothing. You still want to keep this ship in port?"

"No, I guess not."

"I didn't think so."

They keep on walking to the gangway, but I stay where I am. A killer on board? That's why they're here? And my father doesn't know. Should I tell him?

I want to hear more, so I decide to follow the policemen down the gangway. I don't get far. Danilo grabs my shoulder and tells me to follow him. Danilo is the ship's chief steward and before that he was a cook. Now he has four cooks and six mess men under him because *Il Destino* is going to take paying passengers on some of its voyages, and it will be Danilo's job to take care of them.

I've known him for four years, since I was eleven, and he was sixteen. Now he's twenty. He's shorter than me. I'm five-six; he's five-five, maybe five-four. As I follow him, I spot something I've never noticed before: He has a bald patch on the top of his head, right at the back, like a monk.

We've always gotten along. I'd say we're friends, even. But he hasn't acted like my friend since I came on board.

We head to my father's quarters and walk through the chart room between the cabinets with their long, narrow drawers and the blackboard over them. The big heading says, "Soundings," and under it are two other headings, each with a list below it—all in chalk.

The clock on the wall chimes the quarter hour as we go through to my father's office, which is just as narrow as the chart room, and, finally, to his berth. He's standing in front of his bunk, his chin resting on his hands. His fingers are locked together like he's praying. He looks very serious. I mean, more serious than usual, because he always looks serious.

"Sit down, Francesca." It's his most solemn voice, the one he uses when he's going to say something I don't want to hear. Like when he told me I had to stay with my aunt and uncle after Mom died. And I'm right. Because he's telling me that I can't go with him and that I have to go back to Uncle Ronnie and Aunt Bess, at least for now. I thought it was because he found out about the killer, but it isn't.

"This was just delivered by taxi," he says and hands me a letter.

Dear Flavio, I read.

You and Frances left so quickly that I didn't have time to react. Almost as soon as you were out the door, I realized that for a girl as young and vulnerable as Frances to live on a ship without her friends and family would be a disaster.

I look up from the paper and almost shout with anger. "What does this mean, without my family? You are my family!"

"Please finish the letter, Francesca."

You are a good father. I realize that. My sister loved you, and I'm sure she had good reason to do so. However, you know as well as I do that a cargo ship is no place to raise a child.

Who does Uncle Ronnie think he is? Of course, my mother had good reason to love my father. And I'm not a child! I want to tell my father this but I know that if I do, he will think I'm being childish.

If you hadn't realized this, you would have taken Frances with you after Catherine's funeral. I do understand why you feel you have to take her now. My wife and I must have appeared uncaring. But, please, let me assure you that both Bess and I care deeply about Frances, and after we had a long and frank discussion, we decided that the child belongs here, in Baltimore, with her mother's family. The complaints Bess voiced were just words of frustration that Frances's attempts at boarding school did not work out. But Bess realizes now that the best thing for Frances is to be in a stable home environment, with us and our boys.

Therefore, we are asking you to return our niece to our home. We promise to see to her physical and emotional well-being and to ensure that she receives the education and upbringing she deserves and which, I am sure, Catherine would have wished for her.

Your brother-in-law,
Ronald Porter

I finish the letter but don't look up. I'm trying very hard not to lose my temper. I know what's behind my lawyer uncle's letter. He sat quietly while Aunt Bess complained about me, not contradicting her, just like he almost always does. But every once in a while, he surprises Aunt Bess by fighting back. That's what he's doing this time. He feels guilty about sending me away and made my aunt feel guilty, too. So, she gave in and said I could return.

Mom would know what was happening, but not my father. He doesn't know my aunt and uncle like I do.

Finally, I raise my eyes to him. He looks like he's going to cry. He doesn't. Instead, he hugs me, calls me his *Tesoro*, his treasure, and says he loves me and that it is his job as my father to look out for my welfare.

This is all in Italian because that's what my father speaks best. He taught it to me, plus my mother sent me to classes every Saturday at the church in Little Italy to learn it, even though her parents didn't like the idea. So, now, I am really good, *bravissima*, in Italian.

"You won't be looking out for my welfare if you make me live with them," I say into his chest, also in Italian. "Aunt Bess only changed her mind because of Uncle Ronnie, but it won't last long. Something will happen, and she'll get angry at me. And then it will start all over again, and you'll have to come and get me, so I might as well stay here with you now and save you the trip."

"No, Francesca." He stands back from me, his hands squeezing my shoulders. "This time, you will be a good girl and obey your aunt and uncle, understand?"

"Please, Papa. I lost Mom. I don't want to lose you. Please." I force myself not to cry as I say this.

He pulls me back into a hug. "You won't be losing me, *Tesoro*. I will be back as much as possible. I promise."

Before I can say anything else, he lets go of me, lowers his head, pushes his hands through his gray hair and tells me to get my things and meet him on deck by the gangway.

I go but not to where he said to meet him.

CHAPTER 5

The Dodger

He is out of that room and the bodyguard's clutches and on his way to *Il Destino*. Its green, white, and red funnels almost look welcoming, until he's a few hundred feet from the gangway and sees the police cars. They were here earlier and left. Why are they back?

Time to make a decision. Should he approach the ship and climb the gangway like any other seaman returning from shore leave? What if the police are there to make an arrest—to arrest *him*, in fact? But how could they know he was the one who killed the Wiper? There were no witnesses. No, they probably came back to ask the captain and crew some more questions.

Anyway, what other choice does he have? Go back to the boss and tell him he can't board the ship because he might be arrested? That would be signing his own death warrant. Turn around, walk out the gate, and get on a bus to somewhere? The Dodger would need money for that, the money the boss gave him to do this job. But he doesn't have it on him. It's carefully hidden on *Il Destino*.

The ship, then.

Why are the police here?" he asks the chief mate as he reaches the top of the gangway.

"The girl has disappeared."

"The girl?"

"The captain's daughter. I knew it was a stupid idea, a girl on board. Bad luck on ships."

"Girls are bad luck?"

"Sure. Any sailor knows that."

The chief mate looks like he's starting to wonder about the Dodger,

16

so the Dodger lowers his head and walks past him. The police aren't going to be arresting anyone today. They're just looking for a runaway girl.

CHAPTER 6

Frankie

It's pretty scary in the warehouse, but I figure no one will think of looking for me here. Except for the towers of crates I slip in between, it's empty. Well, almost empty. I hear noises, and I'm pretty sure it's rats making them. Ugh!

And now I see them, running across the floor. Please don't let them stop and look at me.

My plan was to wait until *Il Destino* was about to leave port, then sneak back on board and hide below deck somewhere. Now I realize that was a really stupid idea. When I ran off the ship, I was being just what my aunt always accuses me of, impulsive. I didn't stop to think, as she always says. Of course, almost as soon as I snuck into the warehouse, I realized that my father would never leave without knowing where I am and that I'm safe. So, here I am, in a warehouse full of rats, trying to figure out what to say to him when I return to *Il Destino*.

And then I hear another noise. Like someone is shuffling along to slow music but without there actually being music. *Swish, Swish.* Now a gargling sound. And now a spitting sound. Rats don't spit. At least, I don't think they do.

I scrunch up against one of the crates and try to be quiet—like a mouse, not a rat. *Swish. Swish.* It's getting closer. I move to the other side of the crate and squat down. Whatever it is might swish by and not see me. I close my eyes as tightly as I can, but that makes it scarier, so I open them.

And see two legs. Human legs. In dirty pants that smell like he peed in them. When I stand up, I'm looking into two red eyes.

I scream and run.

When I finally stop, I'm deep in the warehouse, and the crates are piled almost to the ceiling. I have no idea where the door is, but at least the man is not around. I know because I can't hear him, and I can't *smell* him.

The rats are still here, though. Them I can hear.

It's so dark I can't even see the shape of the crates. I need to find my way back to the door and to my father. I put my hands out in front of me, so I don't bump into anything, and move forward, like I'm playing Blind Man's Bluff. My hands knock against wood, a crate. I feel my way around it and inch forward again. Another crate. I feel my way around it, too. I feel like I might be stuck in here forever. Will anyone look here? Why should they? And why was I stupid enough to think this was a good idea?

I take tiny steps, but not tiny enough. I stumble and stop myself from falling by reaching my arms out even further. My hands touch something rough, concrete maybe, or bricks. The inside wall of the warehouse? Yes, it must be. I just need to keep my hands on it and follow it until it brings me back around to the door at the front of the warehouse.

I miss my mother. I wish she hadn't died.

I keep moving, slowly, slowly. The warehouse must be huge because it's taking forever. I reach a corner, turn right.

A sound makes me stop. The warehouse door opening. I move faster and so do the rats. One runs over my feet. Its horrible tail rubs against my leg. That's when I scream.

"Francesca?" It's a man's voice but not my father's, so I don't answer.

"Francesca?" the voice calls again. "Francesca, it's the police. We're not going to hurt you, but your father is very worried about you. If you're there, come on out. You need to come with us."

"I'm coming." My voice is shaky and too low, and I hear the policeman say to someone else, "Did you hear something?" I clear my throat and shout, "I'm here. I'm coming."

"I think I hear her," the other man says. By now, I've reached another corner and am much closer to the voices. "It's me. It's Frankie. I'm here." I want to scream, Please don't close the door again, and I start moving faster. There's more light now; I can see the shapes of the crates. I shout again. "I'm coming. Don't leave!"

Just then, I stop dead. A bright light is shining in my face.

"Lower the light, Doyle, so she can see." Doyle lowers his flashlight. It shines on his shoes.

I run right at them.

CHAPTER 7

The Dodger

The captain's daughter has disappeared, and now the crew has to search the ship. Bad luck for them, but good luck for the Dodger. He can look for the document while the rest of the men look for the girl.

He's in one of the cabins reserved for the passengers boarding in New Orleans. No room really for a girl to hide but plenty of room to hide a document. He closes the door so no one sees him searching for it. He can hear shouted commands, so he hurries as much as possible. Once the ship takes on passengers, he won't have another chance to search here.

The shouts and the running feet sound closer. He only has a few minutes. He checks the closet, rubbing his hands along the back and sides to make sure there's nothing taped there; inside all the drawers; and then pulls them out to look behind and below them, trying to steady his hands so he doesn't drop one.

Now, the voices are outside the door. His head swivels around looking for other possible hiding places. Under the mattress. Easy to hide papers there. He pulls it up on its side just as the door opens. He freezes with the mattress clutched in both hands, then turns his head. It's the first mate.

"What are you doing looking under a mattress? How little do you think the captain's daughter is? Small enough to hide under a mattress?" He points his thumb to the door. "Get out of here."

As the Dodger slips past him, he hears him mumble, "Idiot." That word again.

Back on deck, the Dodger watches as the captain's daughter climbs the gangway, a police officer on either side of her. One thing the hunt for

21

her showed him is that finding the document will be a lot harder than he thought. *Il Destino* has cabins and hatches and pipes and holds and tanks, and it could be hidden in any of them. He regrets promising the boss that he would find it by the time the ship docks in the next port. It will only take four days to reach New Orleans. That's not a lot of time.

He looks again at the girl who's on deck with her father. She's hugging him, and he's patting her back.

And he wonders: It's obvious the captain cares for his daughter. How far would he go to save her?

CHAPTER 8

Frankie

I am still in my coat and sweating because there is so much heat coming from the radiator. We're in my father's office. I have my hands behind me, gripping the edge of his desk, and wishing I was in my own cabin or on deck or anywhere else. Well, maybe not in the warehouse.

"Never do that again, Francesca. Never! Do you understand?" I'm used to my aunt and grandparents yelling at me, but this sounds much worse. Maybe because my father's never done it before. Maybe because it's in Italian, so he sounds madder than he really is.

"I'm sorry, Papa. I promise it will never happen again." Please don't send me back, I want to say. Please let me stay with you. Then, I do an embarrassing thing. I cry. My father puts his arms around me and pats my back.

"*Mia povera Francesca, mia povera figlia,*" he whispers. But I don't want to be his *poor* daughter; I just want to be his daughter, so this makes me cry even harder.

Finally, I say what I was only thinking before. "Please, Papa. Please don't send me back."

"Shush, *Tesoro*. I'm not sending you back."

I pull away and look up at his face. "You're not?" I don't ask why, but he answers anyway.

"I don't think it will work, you staying with your aunt and uncle. Your attitude. What might happen if you do go back." He shakes his head. "No, I don't think it is a good idea." He gives me a sad smile and pats my cheek. "We'll work things out when we reach Naples."

I'm so relieved. Then I start to wonder what he means by 'work things out' when we reach Naples.

So, here I am, on deck again, watching the longshoremen loading cargo—lots of crates. I'll have to ask my father what's in them. I'll wait 'til he settles down a little, though. They're also loading Chevys from the plant in Baltimore. Funny to think that the Italians send us little Alfa Romeos and we send them big Chevy Bel Airs.

One of the deckhands, the one who looks like Troy Donahue in that movie Mom took me to, looks up from what he's doing and gives me a big smile. I can't help smiling back. Maybe he doesn't think I look ugly with my chopped-up hair. I heard another deckhand call him Edvard. Edvard looks around—to see if any of the officers could see him, I think—and walks over to me.

"Do you like candy, Miss?"

Wow! He actually talked to me. I can't say anything, I'm so surprised. Also, I've never spoken to someone so good looking before. So, I just nod. Then, he does something that surprises me even more. He tucks a Snickers bar into my hand, winks, and goes back to helping load the cargo.

Papa still doesn't know there's a murderer on board. The Baltimore police told him the Wiper was probably killed in a bar fight. I know that's not what they really think, but I've decided not to say anything. Not yet, anyway. I'll wait until we're safely at sea, maybe even after we leave New Orleans. It's not like I'm lying to my father. If he'd asked me what the police said and I didn't tell him, well, that would be a lie. I'm just not mentioning something I overheard. That's all.

The ship is slowly moving away from the port. I look back and see Baltimore getting farther and farther away. I wonder how long it will be before *Il Destino*—and my father and me—return. It's starting to get dark now. Lights are coming on everywhere—on *Il Destino*, on the other ships in port, and in the distance, all over downtown Baltimore. I can see the

Bromo-Seltzer Tower all lit up. It's beautiful, but now I'm on my new home. So, I say goodbye, but not out loud.

Then I turn around and look ahead.

Danilo is standing next to me. He's been extra quiet since I boarded, not at all like he used to be when Mom and I visited *Il Destino* when it was in port. To get him to talk, I ask him why hardly anyone on board talks to me.

"Because some of the crew think a woman on board brings bad luck."

"But I'm only fifteen."

"In a lot of the places they come from, the father of a girl your age would be looking for a husband for her."

I pull the collar of my coat up around my neck. He does the same to his. "I can't imagine my father doing that."

"I can't either."

Maybe the chief mate is one of the crew who thinks females on board are bad luck. His name is Rocco Garafolo. He's never been nice to me, even before Mom died.

"Danilo, do you think that's why Officer Garafolo hates me so much?"

He pulls away from the rail and turns to look at me. "No. It's probably because he thinks he should be *Il Destino*'s captain. He thinks he has more experience and that your father got the job instead of him because he knows more people in the Home Office."

"Does he? My father, I mean."

"Hasn't he ever talked to you about his job?"

"No. Sometimes my Mom would, but not Papa." Actually, I really don't know my father all that well. Except for a day or two every few months when his ship was in port, he's only been home with my Mom and me two months a year. Danilo knows this since he's been a part of the crew for four years. Then I confess what he doesn't know. "When he was on his two-month leave, it always took me a while to get used to him. He always brought Mom and me presents and took us out to dinner, and it was so nice to be like my friends, having a father at home. Then he was gone again."

Danilo gives that sad smile of his, the first he's given me since I've been on board, then turns back to look at Baltimore receding and leans his elbows against the ship railing. "Your father, Frankie, is the captain because of his experience when he served in the war."

"Even though he was on the wrong side?"

Danilo's smile is less sad. "Yes, even though he was on the wrong side."

"And does my father know more people than Officer Garafolo?"

"No, but none of them like Garafolo, and they all like your father. They know what a good man he is."

Well, as Aunt Bess would say, I don't doubt that.

CHAPTER 9

Frankie

I wake up really early—at five bells, which is 6:30 in the morning. If the bells hadn't woken me, the seamen would have. They're sweeping and mopping the deck and chipping rust and painting, mending canvases and operating winches and other machines I don't know the names of yet. And they're speaking in all kinds of languages, but mostly English and Italian. They speak so fast or with such thick accents that they could be speaking Chinese, and I wouldn't know the difference.

Now, I'm eating dinner in the officer's mess, smaller than the seamen's mess but not really any fancier. The chair seats are green, like the table tops, and are fastened to the floor just like in the seamen's mess. So, this is where I will eat every day.

It's pretty awkward. I'm finding out that it's not only the unlicensed seamen who won't talk to me. The officers won't either. They all have their heads hanging over their plates—so they don't have to look I me, I guess. All except one, Drago Petrovic, the really, really handsome Yugoslavian third mate.

"How was your first day on board, Miss Francesca?" Everyone except Papa and Danilo call me this or sometimes just "Miss." I asked Drago to call me Frankie or even Francesca, but I think even he is a little afraid of my father.

"It was fine. I woke up really early and had breakfast with my father and then studied all morning. Then I had lunch and walked on deck for my recess."

"Recess?"

"A sort of *pausa* that we have at school, only there I have my friends to talk to."

"You miss your friends?"

"Yes. No! I mean I miss them, yes, but I'd rather be here."

Drago nods his head and mumbles, "Of course."

"Anyway," I hurry on," after the *pausa*, I finished my school work and then came here for dinner."

"So, you did a lot of studying. Good girl."

Good girl? Does he think he's my teacher or something? I mean, he's not that much older than me. I get angry at Aunt Bess again for my stupid hairdo. It makes me look like a ten-year-old. Drago probably wouldn't have called me *girl* if my hair was like it used to be.

Still, he's really nice, nicer than anyone else in the officers' mess right now. I hope he always eats dinner at this time. Otherwise, I'm going to be having some pretty quiet meals.

Papa sends for me after dinner to go over my school work. He's sitting at his desk in his office, and I'm in the chair next to it. Papa is especially good at Italian, Geometry, and Geography. He's also good at Italian history, so he quizzes me on that for a long time. He's not as good on American history, except for Christopher Columbus, so I tell him, "You don't have to worry about that, Papa."

"You are half-American, Francesca, so American history is important for you to know. And it's important that you study it for you Mama's sake." He puts his head down and looks at his hands. Since she's died, he's done this every time he mentions her. I want to hug him and tell him not to be sad, but I'm sad, too, so how can he not be sad?

"Don't worry, Papa," I say instead. "I will study American history so hard that you'll have to give me an A." He looks up, smiles and puts his hand on my cheek. A minute later, he's on his way to the bridge. When does he sleep, I wonder?

I don't go to sleep right away. I realize that I don't care about missing my friends or Baltimore. I only want to be with Papa, even if it means that the only people who will talk to me are him, Danilo, and Drago Petrovic. But suppose Papa finds out that whoever killed the Wiper is probably still on *Il Destino*? Will he let me stay here?

No, he won't. I know him well enough to know that he would be afraid that the killer might hurt me. If he finds out, he will send me back to Baltimore. I can't let that happen.

I think I'm the only one on board who knows, so I just have to make sure I don't say anything about it. And if he does find out somehow, I'll just have to find the killer so Papa can lock him up and stop worrying about me.

CHAPTER 10

Frankie

Once I realized that my bathroom was used by some of the officers before I came on board, I thought it might be a good idea to tie the door with some rope—just in case one of them decided to use my bathroom, anyway, and I walked in on them by mistake. That would be so embarrassing.

So, that's what I did last night before I went to bed: I tied a knot around the handle of the bathroom door, then looped it around the fire extinguisher on the wall next to it. Now, I have a problem. I need to go to the bathroom before I go to breakfast, and I can't untie the knot. I'm trying to unravel it, but it's not working. Then, I pull on it, but that makes the knot tighter.

I'm crossing my legs and trying to decide what to do next when a voice behind me says, "Is there a problem, Miss?" I jump and whirl around. It's one of the seamen, Osvaldo. He's from Chile, Danilo told me. He's very tall and has red hair and freckles. I like his smile. How can he move so quietly? I uncross my legs, lean my body against the knot, and hope nothing happens. He peaks around me and sees the knot. Could I be more embarrassed? Yes, if I don't get in the bathroom soon, I could.

"How did that happen?"

Before I can think of an answer, he tells me he will take care of it, so I take a few steps to the side. His hands move easily over the rope and, almost automatically, the knot comes undone.

"There. All fixed. Do you want me to report this to your father? Whoever did this shouldn't have. It's very irresponsible."

"No, no. That's all right. I don't want to get anyone in trouble."

"Well, then," and he gives me a funny smile, "I'll leave you to it."

He walks away, and I race into the bathroom. Next time, I'll just put up a sign.

I'm the last one at the breakfast table this morning. Papa, the second mate, and the purser have all left, leaving me alone. But not really alone; Winston is here. He's tall, too, and handsome. I wonder if you have to be both to get a job on *Il Destino*. But no. Not all the seamen are tall and handsome, just the ones who will talk to me. Winston brings me a second helping of toast and some more orange juice. It's like being in a restaurant with my own private waiter—a friendly waiter who likes to talk and answers all my questions.

"What country do you come from, Winston?"

"Jamaica, Miss."

"In the Caribbean?"

"That's right."

"Do you live on the sea there like here?"

"Close enough to walk." He's looking out the porthole when he says this as if he could see Jamaica through it.

"Do you miss it much?"

"Sometimes. But I like it on *Il Destino*, and not just because I make good money. I like the crew—well, most of them, anyway—and your father is a good boss. Would you like some more orange juice?"

"No, thank you, Winston. I'd better get back to studying."

Osvaldo and Winston and Edvard aren't the only unlicensed seamen who are nice to me. Magnus is, too. He looks like he could be Edvard's younger brother, tall, blonde and really cute. He's from Denmark, I think, and friendly but shy. He always smiles at me and then lowers his eyes like he shouldn't have. Then, he looks up and smiles again. He's the one who helped me hang the pictures on the wall of my cabin. He was shy with me even then. It was very hard to get him to talk. Finally, I gave up trying.

I'm glad I'm getting to know Winston and some of the others, and not just because they're so nice. If I'm going to find the murderer, they'll be able to tell me about the rest of the unlicensed crew. Language isn't a problem; they all speak either English or Italian and sometimes both. Not always well, but good enough.

Danilo can help me with this, I'm sure, so last night I went to the galley to talk to him.

"Danilo, do you think maybe whoever killed the Wiper might be a member of the crew?" I'm leaning against one of the refrigerators in the galley as he inspects the food supplies in the cupboards. I didn't want to tell him what I know for a fact—that the killer is almost sure to be on board—because he might say something to Papa. I thought he'd laugh and say, "Don't be ridiculous, Frankie," or, "A girl your age shouldn't think about things like that." But his reaction really surprised me. He slammed a cupboard door shut, whipped around and glared at me.

"There are more important things in life to worry about than a non-existent killer." Then he brushed past me and left the galley.

Should I have told him what I overheard the police lieutenant say? Maybe later, when Danilo is in a better mood.

CHAPTER 11

The Dodger

The search for the document is definitely not as easy as the Dodger thought it would be. Every part of the ship seems to be constantly manned. He's looked in the Wiper's old bunk, in his locker, in the lockers of the other engine room crew. No document. It's vital that he find it. If he doesn't—no, he will not think of that. He will find it, and his country will continue to prosper under the Leader.

He knows that the Wiper wouldn't have hidden it in such obvious places, but he had to look, just in case. On the other hand, the hiding place had to be easy for the Wiper to get to, so he could stash it without being seen. The Wiper couldn't roam the ship at will any more than the Dodger can. So, where on this boat could a Wiper be without drawing attention to himself?

One place is the mess and, if no one was around to see him, the galley. The Dodger heads to the mess. The last two times he tried, he couldn't look for the document because there was always at least one seaman there. Time to try again.

There are four men there when he arrives—Winston, a steward; Nello, the chief cook; and two of the mess men. They're sitting 'round a table, a coffee mug in front of each of them, cigarettes dangling from their mouths and an array of playing cards between them. Gambling—in the Dodger's opinion, another example of the decadence of these people.

The steward and the others are laughing. The four of them could sit here for hours playing their stupid card game if they feel like it. The Dodger decides to try again much later, when it's sure to be empty.

The mess is empty now, and no one should be coming in until it's time for the cook to start breakfast. That leaves the Dodger plenty of time to search both the mess and the galley.

The mess itself is easy enough. The only places a document could be hidden so that it's not found by accident is taped under the table or under the chairs and even then, someone might discover it. But the Dodger has to look. He rubs his hand under each chair. He doesn't find the document, but does find stale chewing gum.

He gets on his knees to check the table's underside and the corners where the legs join the top. Nothing there. He's about to rise when one of the mess men walks in.

The Dodger jumps up too quickly and knocks his head against a corner of the table.

"I can't find my knife," he lies. "I thought I might have dropped it when I was eating."

"Did you find it?"

"No."

"You'd better, and quick before the first mate finds out." It sounds like friendly advice.

"Yeah, I know. I'd better check my bunk again." The Dodger steps around him.

"Good luck."

The Dodger steps into the companionway. The galley will have to wait.

CHAPTER 12

Frankie

My father is not happy with me. Again. He saw me talking to Osvaldo. Apparently, because he's not an officer, Osvaldo is off limits to me. I wonder if all Italians are this snobby.

We're in my father's cabin. The only things on the wall are a clock, smaller than the one in the chart room, a large map of the world with lots of crisscrossing lines on it, and a picture of a man with a long, white beard and a big book and pole in his hands. It's St. Elmo, the patron saint of sailors, my father says. Mom told me a long time ago that Papa isn't very religious for an Italian, but that he insisted that she take me to church every Sunday. That's another thing Aunt Bess didn't approve of—Mom taking me to a Catholic Church when there was a perfectly good Methodist church not far from our house.

Anyway, the only other picture is in a frame on the table next to his bunk, the same one I have on the wall in my cabin, a photo of the three of us—Papa, Mom, and me when I was still little enough for Mom to carry. It's not in color, but you can tell that my father's hair is dark, not gray, and Mom's is dark blonde like mine. His arm is around her shoulder, and the tops of their heads are almost touching, they are leaning so close to each other. My father isn't looking at the camera. He's looking at the two of us. Mom always called it our "Three Bears" picture. That's why when I was little, I never wanted to be Goldilocks. Back then, I just wanted to be the baby bear.

I turn my head back and ask my father a question.

"If I'm not supposed to talk to the ordinary seamen, what about Winston and the other mess men? How am I going to tell them what I want to eat?" It's probably not a good idea to ask the last question. It sounds sarcastic. If I can't talk to Winston and Edvard and Osvaldo and

Magnus, the only people who are friendly to me except for Drago on this entire ship, who will I talk to? Just my father and Danilo and Drago? So, although I was mad when I asked that question, I wish I could take it back. Then, when my father replies, I realize that maybe in Italian it didn't sound so sarcastic because he's not angry.

"Of course, you can talk to the men who work in the mess and anybody else when you have to. But only if you need to, understand?"

"Yes, Papa, I understand." Before I can say something about wanting to re-check my Geometry because that would impress him, he stands up, puts out his hand for mine, and tells me he will see me at dinner.

On the way back to my cabin, it occurs to me that I'll probably have to talk to lots of crew members while I'm on the ship for one reason or another. A deckhand, for instance, if—what? I'm sure there will be a reason. Oh, I'll think of one. By the time I sit down at my desk, I'm smiling.

Maybe I won't be so lonely, after all.

I'm about to walk into my father's office so we can go to dinner together when I see he's with Danilo, so I stay outside and look through the small opening in the door. Mom would never approve of me eavesdropping like this, but how else can I find out what's going on?

Danilo places a mug of coffee on my father's desk.

"You're a lucky man to have so much family, Danilo. There is always someone there you can count on if you need to."

"Are you worried about Francesca, Captain? She seems to be settling in here. And most of the crew have started to accept her."

"She has settled in, Danilo. That's not the problem. I received a radio call from the police in Baltimore last night. They think that the Wiper was murdered by one of the ship's crew." He takes a sip of his coffee. Danilo brews it strong like Papa wants it.

"How do they know that?"

"The lieutenant says they found a witness who saw the Wiper with someone from *Il Destino*."

"But how could they tell? That the person was from here, I mean?"

"The witness says that later he saw the man boarding the ship."

"Who's the witness?"

"A longshoreman who didn't know about the murder until he read it in the newspaper. He'd been off work sick, so he wouldn't have heard about it from the others."

"Did he describe him?" Now, he decides to be curious, not like when I hinted about the killer to him.

"It's not much of a description. The longshoreman said he was wearing a ski cap, so he couldn't tell what color his hair was. He wasn't even sure about his size. Not very helpful."

"And that's why Francesca has to leave the ship? Even if the Home Office says she can stay on board?" Danilo asks.

Please, Papa, don't send me back. I want to rush into his office and say that, but I can't, not without his finding out I was eavesdropping.

"Yes. When we reach New Orleans. We don't know why this person killed the Wiper. Maybe they were drunk and had a fight, or one of them owed the other money and wouldn't pay it. He might never kill again, but I can't take that chance with my daughter."

No, Papa would never take that chance.

But I can't go back to Baltimore. I won't. I have to find a way to change Papa's mind, but how?

By finding the man who killed the Wiper, that's how. Then my father could have him arrested, and there wouldn't be a reason for me to leave the ship. But that's tough to do between now and when we reach New Orleans. And where do I start?

CHAPTER 13

The Dodger

H is boss swore that someone would be waiting in the French Quarter the next day to receive the document, but there's no document for the Dodger to hand over, at least not yet.

He keeps asking himself where it could be. Every chance he's had—and there haven't been many because there are crew members everywhere and all the time—he had no luck. He can't look now because he has to help with the unloading as soon as *Il Destino* docks. This will take all day, all day in the rain though it will give him another chance to search the cargo holds, if only briefly. That means he only has tonight to find it. And if he doesn't find it, he will have to deliver the news to whomever the boss has sent—he dreads that it might be the bodyguard—and then never leave New Orleans alive.

Just then, the captain's daughter marches by. To him, she always looks like she's marching in a parade. He forces himself to smile at her when she smiles and waves.

Then his smile becomes genuine as he gets an idea. If he can't find the document by tomorrow, he's thought of another plan. If he can get the girl off the ship and into the hands of his boss's henchman, then the Dodger can persuade—no, force—the captain to make his crew look for the document. A couple of pieces of paper in exchange for his daughter's life? That's a bargain the captain will surely make.

CHAPTER 14

Frankie

Today, it's drizzling, not raining hard like yesterday when the deck-hands were unloading the cargo. I'm waiting on deck for Papa, trying to think about spending the day with him and not about saying goodbye to him at the airport.

"Francesca." I spin around to find Danilo just inches behind me.

"The captain wants to see you in his quarters." He makes it sound as though I'm going to be court martialed. Do they court martial people in the Italian Merchant Marine? Danilo has gotten so crabby since we left Baltimore that I'm almost convinced that is what's going to happen.

When we get to my father's quarters, I'm about to walk in when Danilo grabs my arm, a little too hard, and pulls me back. Then he knocks on the door and opens it when my father shouts, "*Avanti.*"

"Your daughter, Captain."

What's going on? Danilo's never done this before, introduced me like he was a nurse and I was a patient there to see some important doctor who's about to give me bad news, like I only have twenty-four hours to live.

Papa points to the chair by his desk. "Francesca, sit down, please." Following orders—maybe this is a court martial, after all—I sit down on the only other chair in his office.

"I know I promised I would take you into New Orleans today."

"Yes, Papa. Don't worry about the weather. I have my raincoat," I hold my arms out to the side, so he can see it with his own eyes. "I'm all ready when you are." But he has that look on his face. I hate, really hate, that look—the "I'm afraid I have bad news for you" look. It seems to me that it's my father's favorite expression. For me, anyway. I know what's coming. He can't take me into the city. And I'm right.

"I can go on my own, just like I always did in Baltimore."

"Absolutely not. You don't know New Orleans."

"Well, then, how about another officer—or one of the seamen?"

"No, *Carina*. You don't know the officers well enough, and the rest of the crew …" He shrugs, which in this case means I should realize I'm not supposed to be spending time with a non-officer. "No, you will go with Danilo."

I start to argue again, but he stops me with a swipe of his hand across his chest. I'm starting to wonder if it's so great to have a father who is not only a strict Italian but a snob as well.

As soon as I think this, I feel guilty. When Mom and I flew over to visit him in Livorno, we stayed in his apartment. It's up sixty-five steps in a building that has no elevator and is so old I thought it was from Roman times. But the stairs aren't the worst part. The worst part is how small his apartment is, with a kitchen and living room and dining room combined not much bigger than my old bedroom. And I can't describe the bathroom in his apartment because there isn't one. Only a sink. Everything else, the bathtub and the toilet, are down the hall and shared by the people in two other apartments. I didn't know what to think.

"Is Papa poor?" I asked Mom.

"No, Sweetie, not poor. Your Papa lives here so he can send most of his salary to us," she told me. "That's why we can live in a nice house and you can have your own room."

So, I guess it doesn't matter if he's strict. And I don't care anymore about his being a snob. I put that down to his not being American.

But I'm still not happy about going ashore with Danilo.

My stomach is growling because I didn't eat breakfast this morning. We were going to have breakfast in the French Quarter and eat what they call *beignets*. Papa says they're pretty good even if they aren't made in Italy.

I wait in my cabin until Danilo comes to get me. I re-check my school work for the hundredth time, check my suitcase to make sure I haven't forgotten anything, then smooth out the blanket on my bunk, which I messed up when I put the suitcase on it.

I'm looking forward to trying the beignets, but I'm not looking forward to going with Danilo. It's strange. He's the only non-officer Papa trusts enough to let me leave the ship with, and he's always been nice, though he often looks like his dog just died. I've known him for years, and we've always gotten along. But lately he's been acting odd, really weird. He always used to answer all my questions about his home and his family and his fiancée and his plans. But on the way from Baltimore, that changed. Now he's always distracted, and he hasn't paid any attention to me. And when he does, it's only to look at me like he's wondering who I am.

Still, if I want to see New Orleans, going with Danilo is the only way.

We're walking along Market Street. I studied a map of this part of the city before we docked, so I know exactly where we are and where we should be heading to get our beignets. But that's not where he's taking me.

"Danilo, this isn't the way to the Café du Monde."

"Not now. I have to make a call first."

"A call? Can't you do that later? I'm hungry." I don't mean for it to come out like a whine, but I think it did. As I say, I'm hungry.

"You'll get your beignets after I make this call." He's walking so fast that I have to run to keep up with him even though he's shorter than I am.

I wouldn't mind being on my own in New Orleans, but the thing is, I didn't study this part on the map, so I have no idea where we are, only that we're on a small street, almost an alley. There are no signs, no restaurants, nothing but two- and three-story buildings with little iron balconies hanging over our heads.

I'm hurrying to keep up when Danilo swerves into a building on our right. A bell clangs as he opens the door and enters. I follow him.

The inside is so dark, it takes a while for me to make out what it is. It must be some kind of food store, because there are a lot of cans on shelves, but the labels aren't in English. There's a light at the other end of the room through a doorway covered by rows of beads hanging to the floor. As my eyes adjust to the darkness, I see that no one else is here.

Danilo stops suddenly and calls out something. I don't know what because it isn't in either of my languages. I guess it's Filipino, if that's what it's called. An old woman comes through the beaded curtain and into the room. Her gray hair is pulled back so tightly that it's a wonder that she doesn't have a headache. She's wearing a long, faded black dress that covers her whole body except for her hands and feet. She's not smiling, and she doesn't look at me, only at Danilo. Suddenly, she nods at him, turns, and goes back through the curtain of beads. Danilo starts to follow her.

"Danilo!"

He turns around. I think he forgot I was there. I wish he had, actually, rather than look at me the way he does now. I don't like this.

"Stay here, Francesca. I will only be five minutes." And then he, too, disappears behind the curtain.

I look around. I see two small iron tables with a few white plastic chairs around them. It's very quiet. The only thing I hear is some thumping. It's my heart. I put a shaky hand up to my chest to try to slow it down or make it quieter, but that doesn't work.

Minutes pass and then more minutes. Why am I so scared? Is it because I can't figure out what this place is? Because it's so dark in here? Because Danilo has been gone so long? Because that woman is so foreign looking?

No, it's because now I know why Danilo's been acting the way he has lately. Now that I've had a chance to think about it, I realize when his mood got really bad—when I tried to tell him that the police thought the killer was probably a member of *Il Destino*'s crew. And the only reason I can think of why that would make him angry is if he's actually the one who killed the Wiper. What other reason could there be? I've done nothing to make him mad at me; I'm sure of that. So, it must be that he realized he was no longer safe from being caught, that now the police and my father would be looking at everyone on the ship to see who could have done it. That's most likely when he decided he had to get rid of me. So, he brought me here.

And stupid me for trusting him, for telling him I wanted to find the killer. No, it wasn't stupid of me to trust him. Not at all. He's been my friend for all these years, or at least that's what I thought. But I was wrong. He was never my friend.

I feel like crying, but I can't. I've got to get away. This place, whatever it is, looks like the kind of place that, when someone walks in the front door, they never walk out.

Well, that's not going to happen to me. There's only one thing to do. I turn around and run out to the street.

CHAPTER 15

The Dodger

Early the next morning, the Dodger watches as the first and third mates are the first off the ship, followed by the radio officer and purser. Then the rest of the off-watch crew walk down the gangway, laughing and planning their day in one of their favorite ports. The Dodger is the only one not laughing and the only one not planning. He knows that when he gets off the ship, someone, whatever goon the boss has sent, will be waiting, and he will have to explain that he doesn't have the document because he can't find it.

Unless …

Unless he can use the back-up plan he thought of yesterday—grab the girl and turn her over to the goon, who can hold her while the Dodger makes the captain order his crew to search for the document. The captain would do that for his daughter. He seems to be that type of father, the kind that likes his daughter.

There is one problem. How can he get her away from the ship and from that Filipino who is always by her side? As he asks himself this question, the two walk past and descend the gangway.

He follows.

Twenty minutes later, the girl and the Filipino go into some sort of shop. The Dodger slips into a doorway at the end of the block. He doesn't have to wait long. Suddenly, the captain's daughter dashes out of the shop. He's about to walk up to her and say hello. She smiles at him enough on the ship. He's sure she has a crush on him; most females do. If the chief steward isn't around, he can coax her into going with him, tell her he's on his way to get a cup of coffee, that he knows a good place and if she's hungry, they have delicious pastries.

But that idea is nixed when she turns to the right, in the opposite direction from where he's hiding, and starts to run. He follows her.

At the next corner, she turns right. He runs after her, but when he gets to that corner, she's nowhere in sight. When he reaches the next corner, he looks left; she's not there. Then in the other direction, and there she is. She's reached a major street.

How did her legs carry her that far, that fast? He sprints after her, but it's too late. She's jumped onto a streetcar, and he's too far behind to jump on after her. He keeps running, hoping the streetcar will come to another stop and he'll be able to catch up with it. But it doesn't. After three blocks, he stops and leans over, hands on his knees, and tries to breathe deeply, but the exercise, or maybe fright at what awaits him if he can't produce the document, makes it difficult to do anything but wheeze.

And then he hears a car stop next to him. When he looks up, he sees it's a taxi, an empty one. He pulls open the door and plops down in the back, the knees of his long legs pushing against the driver's seat. The driver looks at him in the rearview mirror for a few seconds before asking, "Where to?"

The Dodger points to the streetcar, now almost four blocks away, and pants out, "Follow that streetcar." The driver laughs. Then he puts the taxi into gear, and they take off.

CHAPTER 16

Frankie

E ven though I don't look back, I can feel Danilo is there. I can hear his footsteps running behind me, so I run even faster around two corners until I reach a streetcar that's stopped at the intersection. I jump through the exit door. The driver doesn't see me.

I'm not sure how it works here in New Orleans. Do I pay when I get on? Does a conductor come around to take my money or punch a ticket? I'm only sure that if I walk up to the driver from the back of the streetcar, he's going to wonder how I got on and might throw me off. I can't chance that, not until I'm so far enough away from Danilo that he can't catch me.

It's crowded, and the ride is bumpy, almost like a roller coaster without the ups and downs. I scrunch down in one of the wooden seats in the back so the driver doesn't notice me. Everyone else does, though. They look curious, sort of a what's-that-girl-doing-on-our-streetcar kind of look. I just smile at them, and some of them smile back. Then I look out the window.

Some of the houses we're passing are skinny, with only a front door and a window next to it and no top floor. Others are wider but still no top floor, and every once in a while, we pass a big house with pillars out front. None of the houses are row houses like in Baltimore or the French Quarter; they're not connected. Some of them are blue or pink, some green or yellow, along with white. A lot of them need a new paint job. And the streets are wider than the French Quarter, especially the one we're on now.

The different-looking houses don't bother me, but the street names do. I've never heard names like these before. It's like I'm in a foreign country. Names like Barrone, Galvez, Tonti, Villere, Miro, Rocheblave, Prieur—I can't even pronounce some of them.

Should I get off at the next stop? Danilo couldn't have followed me this far. I look around at the other passengers again. The only passenger looking at me is an old lady with a lap full of shopping bags. She smiles gently at me, and I smile back. The rest are staring out a window or reading, and two have their eyes closed. Some are standing up, ready to get off at the next stop. Maybe I should get off with them. I decide against it. I don't know why. I do the same at the next stop. And the next.

Then, the lady who smiled at me starts gathering up her shopping bags, stops to look at me, and says something. I have no idea what it is. They have strong accents, these New Orleans people. Maybe this really is a foreign country.

I start to ask her to repeat what she'd said when everybody else gets up, too. I guess it's the end of the line. I was thinking of staying on it and going back to the French Quarter, but the driver just noticed me and is coming my way.

So, I jump up and hop out the back door, right on the heels of the nice lady who told me that the streetcar wasn't going any farther—if that's really what she said. She turns around and says something else. I can't make that out either. She points behind me. When I look around, I catch a glimpse of someone, a man, I think, disappearing behind an old red Buick convertible parked in front of a grocery store. Danilo? When I turn back to her, she says something about a man and that he was looking at me. She says this slowly so I can understand.

It *is* Danilo.

Now, the driver looks like he's coming after me. I can't stay on this side of the street, not with Danilo waiting for me. I circle around the nice lady, hop over some railroad tracks, and cross the street in front of me, not waiting for the light to change. I don't even look at the street name. It's probably as foreign sounding as the rest of the street names in this city and even if it isn't, I still wouldn't know where I am.

CHAPTER 17

The Dodger

T he cab pulls up behind the streetcar when it stops and everyone starts to get off. The driver asks twice if the Dodger wants to get out here and twice he tells him *yes*. The driver shrugs as he takes the Dodger's money, then makes a U-turn and heads back in the direction of the French Quarter.

The girl has her back to the Dodger. She's talking to an old woman weighed down with shopping bags. The woman notices him and turns back to the girl to say something. He ducks down behind a car before the girl can see him. Then regrets it. There's nothing wrong with his being here. He can think of some reason why he is and then ask the girl where she's going and if he can go with her.

Too late, he stands up and sees the girl running across the street, ignoring the cars going in both directions.

Since the woman who was talking to her is looking at him, he can't run after her, not right away. The streetcar driver is looking, too. The Dodger strolls past them, hands in his pockets, like it's the most natural thing in the world for him to be strolling through their neighborhood. It doesn't work; he can tell by the way they're staring at him, like they're not sure why he's there and what they should do with him.

Still, he keeps walking, faster and faster, up the road where the girl ran around the corner. He sees her a block away, turning at the next corner. He breaks into a run.

This time, he swears she's not getting away.

The houses he passes are small and made of wood. Most are white; some, other colors—blue, brown, yellow. He takes in the peeling paint, the patchy grass in front of some, and the freshly painted ones with flowering bushes in their front yards. For him, both kinds are just more proof of the decadence of this country. In his country, the Leader does not allow houses to become dilapidated. And no one wastes their money on unnecessary things like flowers.

On his right is a wooden church next to a vacant lot surrounded by a chain-link fence. And, everywhere, people, some hurrying but most just strolling along like they have all the time in the world, all of them slowing him down.

Finally, he's catching up with her. If he calls out to her, if she sees it's him, someone from her father's ship, he's sure she'll stop. The Dodger could say he saw her running. What's the problem? Can he help? How could she possibly know what he wants from her?

But what if he's wrong and she hears him and still keeps going, what will all these people think? An adult man running after a teenager? No. He will catch up with her first.

Now, he's almost caught up to her. She's just half a block away, passing what looks like another church and turning another corner. Before he can get to that corner, however, a crowd of women troop out of the church and onto the sidewalk. They stop to talk to each other. The gossiping old fools are blocking his way—blocking everyone's way. He steps into the street. A car honks, and the man behind the wheel yells at him. He doesn't know what because his English isn't good enough to understand the people in this city. But he guesses the meaning from the driver's face and the rude gesture he makes with his hand.

The Dodger turns back and swerves around the women, then turns the corner. The girl is not there. At the next corner, he glances left and right and sees her just as she turns a corner a block away and disappears from his view.

CHAPTER 18

Frankie

The streets are flat. That makes it easier for me to run. It also makes it easier for Danilo to catch up with me. I can feel him closing in, just as I felt it when we were in the French Quarter. I can hear his feet beating on the pavement just as mine are. I can't see him, though, because I'm afraid to turn around.

I keep running around corner after corner after corner. Most of the streets are wide. Some have pavements, and some don't. I run out into the street on the ones that don't and just hope I don't get knocked down by a car. I pass small houses and medium-sized houses, a white wooden church with singing voices coming from its open front doors, a vacant lot with a chain-link fence around it. I run past corner stores too fast to read their signs. I run past women pushing babies in strollers, past men in undershirts digging up the street, past old people walking about a mile an hour. All the women wear dresses and have their hair pinned up or rolled around the backs of their necks or hidden by scarves.

People yell at me as I pass.

"Watch where you're going!"

"What's your hurry, kiddo?"

"Excuse me," I yell back when I bump into one of them. Or, "Have to catch a streetcar." But I stop answering them because I have to save my breath.

I wish Mom were here, pulling up beside me in her car. "Get in," she'd say. And I would, and I'd be safe.

Another corner. I turn it and on my right is a store. There's a sign in front that I don't have time to read. I leap up the three steps to the wood porch and yank open the screen door. It slams behind me. Inside, there's a man with a Santa Claus belly and skin the color of the maple syrup I put on my pancakes. He's standing behind a counter with a glass display case underneath. In front of the counter is a thin woman in a cotton print dress and a little girl with her arms around the woman's left leg. They turn and stare at me.

I'm panting like a dog on a ninety-degree day. And I can't speak because I can't stop panting.

The man comes out from behind the counter. He has snowy white hair ringing his scalp, and he's wearing a white apron blotted with dark stains . He must be a butcher, and the stains must be animal blood because behind him, the display case is full of raw meat. There are even pigs' feet.

The man walks up to me and asks what's wrong. I try to catch my breath so I can answer, but it's hard. I nod, which doesn't really answer his question, I know, but it seems to satisfy him.

The woman walks over to me, too, the little girl still hanging onto her leg. They both have big brown eyes with long eyelashes, like my father's. She takes my arm and leads me to an old wicker chair sitting to the left of the counter. I fall into it and nod again. The man and the woman are looking down at me, and the little girl is looking up. She reaches to touch my skirt, but her mother—I guess it's her mother—pulls her arm back.

Now, I've got my breath back, and I can talk.

"I'm sorry. I don't mean to bother you but—"

But what? What can I tell them? That I'm being chased by a short Filipino who has already murdered one person and now wants to murder me? They might have trouble believing that. Well, at least, I can tell them part of the truth.

"There's a man following me. He's been chasing me all the way from the French Quarter."

The two adults glance at each other. The little girl still stares at me.

"It's true. I live on a ship."

Both adults raise their eyebrows at that.

"My father is the captain. It's an Italian ship, and it's in port right now, and I need to get back there. I'll be safe there."

They look at each other again. The woman whispers something to the man. He nods and goes behind the counter and through a door.

"Josie," I hear him yell. He walks back to the front part of the store, followed by another woman. This one looks old enough to be the mother of the woman with the little girl. She has gray hair folded into a stiff wave, and she's wearing a housecoat like Mom used to wear when she cleaned. The man whispers something to her, and she whispers something back, shaking her head from side to side. I hear the words "crazy" and "dangerous" and wonder if they're talking about me. Finally, he says, "I've got to," unties his apron and hands it to her.

What does he "got to" do? I wonder.

CHAPTER 19

The Dodger

One street runs east and west, the other north and south. She's not on either of them. It's like she fell through a crack in the sidewalk or was pulled up into the clouds. He glances around a second time. It's a street full of houses, with a tavern on one corner and another white, wood church directly across from it.

The girl is still nowhere in sight.

Now he has to make a decision. Does he show up for his meeting empty-handed? Does he keep looking for the girl? Or does he skip the meeting, return to the ship, continue his search, and hope he finds the document before *Il Destino* reaches Naples?

There's another alternative. He brought his money this time. He could catch a bus, not to the port, to someplace else, another city he can lose himself in, someplace where his boss and the rest of them won't be able to find him. Is there such a place? There's a good chance he can get out of New Orleans before they know he's gone. To California. Los Angeles, maybe, or San Francisco.

He immediately rejects the first option, showing up for the meeting. It's not that he's a coward, he assures himself. He's not. He proved that during the war and again during the revolution. But why take unnecessary risks? Why risk a beating—or worse—when there's still a chance he'll find the document? And if he does find it, he can go home. He will have proven himself to the Leader, who will recognize the Dodger's efforts for the revolution. Then, he hopes, he will become one of the Leader's trusted aides.

As far as continuing his search for the girl, it's futile and now he knows it. She could be anywhere in this neighborhood. Anywhere in New Orleans. She could even be on her way back to the ship.

He pulls himself into an erect military stance and tells himself that he cannot forget who he is—at fourteen, one of the youngest soldiers in the Ostvolk, the recipient of the Ostvolk Medal First Class, and now a trusted aide to a trusted aide of the Leader. No. He will not turn his back on the revolution. He will not sacrifice the Leader and the future of his country. He has never been a coward, and he will not start being one now.

He must concentrate on that, return to the ship, continue his search for the document.

He keeps walking, hoping to retrace his steps to where the streetcar stopped. On the way, he passes a five and dime store, a drugstore, and a butcher shop, then turns into the next street on his left.

CHAPTER 20

Frankie

The people in New Orleans are so nice. Turns out what the man *had* to do was take me back to the ship and to my father—even though his wife didn't want him to. When I ask him why she was upset, he says something about my being a white girl and him being a colored man and you never know what people will think.

When we pull up at the gate to the port, I ask him to come with me so my father can thank him. He says, "I'd best not." I like that expression. I think I'll use it some time.

I thank him for myself and for my father. Then I tell him that he saved my life. I don't think he believes that last part, but that's all right. I know it's true.

Ahead of me is *Il Destino*. She's never looked more beautiful—her black hull and white gunwales, the funnels painted red, white, and green, the colors of the Italian flag. I'm tired of running, but afraid Danilo might have caught up with me and still be following me. I know that's not possible, but "I'd best not" take any chances. So, I hurry up the gangway, my eyes on each step. When I reach the top, I look up and see my father.

Standing next to him is Danilo.

CHAPTER 21

Frankie

66 What were you thinking? What were you doing? Danilo says you just disappeared."

As bad as my father's anger is, the look on Danilo's face is worse. It's saying, "I thought you were my friend." It's saying, "I thought you trusted me." It's asking, "Why did you run away from me?"

I can't tell either of them the truth. Not after I found out that Danilo couldn't have been following me because he's been on the ship with my father all the time I was being chased around New Orleans. So, I lie. I think I've never lied as much in my life as I have since I came to live on *Il Destino*.

"It was dark in the room where I was waiting for Danilo, and it was hard to breathe. And I was hungry, so I thought I'd just look around outside, see if there was some place I could get something to eat, you know. Then I got lost." I shrug the Italian shrug. They have no idea how lost I was, and they'll never find out, not if I can help it.

I look at my father, then at Danilo. "I'm sorry." It must be the hundredth time I've said that in the last hour. All I want to do is go to my cabin and curl up on my bunk until it's time to leave for the airport and pretend today never happened. After more questions and lots of warnings, I'm allowed to do that.

It's only when I reach my cabin door that it hits me. If it wasn't Danilo following me in New Orleans, who was it? Because someone was following me. I'm sure of that.

I'm curled up on my bed, just like I was wishing I could be when Papa was yelling at me and Danilo was looking so hurt, when there's a knock on my door. But I'm so depressed, I don't bother to get up. "Come in," I call out. Anyone could walk in, even whoever was following me in New Orleans. But I don't care.

It's Papa. I jump off the bed and stand up straight, like I'm one of the seamen waiting for the captain's inspection.

"Francesca."

"Yes, Papa?"

"While you were in New Orleans, I went ashore to make a phone call."

What's coming next, I wonder. Could anything be worse than going back to my aunt and uncle's house? Is he going to send me to a convent where I won't be allowed to talk and have to get up at 5 o'clock in the morning?

"I've decided that I won't send you back to Baltimore. You will stay on the ship with me." I abandon my seaman-inspection position and throw my arms around him.

He leans back and looks me in the eyes.

"No more running away. No more disappearing. Is that understood?"

"Yes, Papa. I'll be so good. I promise I'll be no trouble at all. You won't be sorry. I promise."

He nods, kisses me on the forehead, and leaves.

He didn't say why he changed his mind, but I can make a guess. I'm sure the phone call was to my Uncle Ronnie. And maybe—no, probably—Aunt Bess answered the phone and said, "You definitely cannot bring Frances back."

So, the only place I'll be is aboard *Il Destino*. Now, definitely, no more cousins sticking chewing gum under the coffee table and blaming it on me. No more aunt nagging me to pull my skirt down. (Actually, my Mom used to do that, too.) And no more grandparents with their constant, "Quiet, Child, I can't hear myself think." I've always thought that was a stupid saying. No one "hears" themselves think.

And I'm finally getting used to living on a ship. My walking is steadier. According to Winston, I've gotten my "sea legs." When he said that, I pictured a mermaid.

Sure, I get seasick sometimes, but much less than before, only when there's a storm or rough seas. Most of the time I feel fine. Sure, I get bored with no TV. But I wasn't allowed to watch TV at my aunt and uncle's house, either. And I could never be as bored as I was there. Never. Sure, I miss being with my friends. But I wasn't with them when I was at boarding school, and I can write them, send them letters and postcards from every port.

And I'll make new friends. Some place. Some day.

But for now, I have a killer to find. Papa must be sure that I am safe on *Il Destino*, and he will never feel that way as long as he thinks the man who murdered the Wiper is on board.

So, where do I start?

CHAPTER 22

The Dodger

It wasn't so hard for him, deciding to return to the ship. And this time the Dodger is sure he will find the document. He just needs to find a taxi to take him back to the port and make sure the taxi drives nowhere near the warehouse where the boss's man is waiting for him.

He looks around. There are no taxis, just a group waiting, probably for the streetcar that the captain's daughter took to get here. He walks over to them, not too close. Only some of them look at him. Maybe they wonder why he's sweating so much when it's not hot. Maybe they think he doesn't belong there.

Well, he doesn't, he tells himself. He doesn't belong in this neighborhood. He doesn't belong in this city. He doesn't belong in this country. He belongs in his own country and, if it weren't for the Wiper's treachery in stealing the document, that's where he would be. The Wiper was on the wrong side in the war and the wrong side in the revolution.

The streetcar arrives, and the group standing apart from the Dodger gets on. He follows. He pulls out a dollar bill and hands it to the driver. The driver presses down on a contraption on his belt and out comes coins, which he hands back. As the Dodger walks to the back of the streetcar, he feels that all eyes are on him. But once he sits down in the last seat, no one turns around.

He gets off in the French Quarter, at the same stop where the captain's daughter jumped on, and walks toward the port. He walks fast since it will be dark soon.

As he approaches the gate to the port, someone steps out, blocking his way. The bodyguard.

The Dodger doesn't resist. The bodyguard doesn't even have to grab the Dodger's arm. The Dodger swears he won't let the bodyguard think that he's afraid of him. He retains his military posture, looks the body-guard in the eye and, imitating the taxi driver, asks, "Where to?"

"Where to" is the warehouse nearest the gate on the wharf, only 150 yards from *Il Destino*. The bodyguard pushes him through the small entrance set inside the large pull-down door, pushes hard enough to make the Dodger stumble into the gloom of the interior. But the Dodger doesn't fall. Maybe that's a mistake; maybe that irritates the bodyguard because that is when he grabs the Dodger's right arm and swings him around, fist raised, ready to smash in his teeth. Then he stops himself and shoves the Dodger farther into the warehouse. This time, the shove sends the Dodger to the floor. It smells of tobacco and grease and rotten fish.

"Up!"

The Dodger pulls himself into a kneeling position and starts to stand. But he takes too long for the bodyguard, who yanks the Dodger's arm up, almost wrenching it from its socket, and drags him across the floor to a metal folding chair barely wide enough to hold him.

The bodyguard squats down in front of the Dodger. His face is almost close enough for the Dodger to taste the fried oysters the bodyguard had for lunch. The bodyguard tilts the Dodger's chin up in an almost affectionate gesture and smiles. Not a reassuring smile. Maybe it's the three missing teeth or the greenish color of the remaining ones. Maybe it's because the bodyguard wears that smile every time he has to beat someone. Either way, the Dodger holds his breath and tightens his stomach muscles, waiting for the blow to come.

It never does. Instead, the bodyguard peers into the Dodger's eyes and starts the questions.

"Where have you looked?"

"Not everywhere yet. There hasn't been enough time."

"Did you check where he slept, where he kept his belongings?"

"They were the first places I looked."

"Where he worked?"

"Not yet. There's too many people around. But I will." It will be the last place he'll look, but he doesn't tell the bodyguard this. The body-guard straightens up and looks down at him.

"We'll give you more time, the time it takes for the ship to reach

Naples. If you don't find the document in those twelve days, the boss says to make sure you jump overboard. That way, we won't have to kill you." He stares into the Dodger's eyes and pulls his arm back. The Dodger tightens his stomach muscles again, but the raised arm doesn't swing around to whack him. Instead, the bodyguard raises it and pats his head—as if the Dodger were a naughty little boy who has been forgiven.

The bodyguard straightens up. "Go back to the ship. Find the document. The Leader must have it, do you understand?" Then, he walks away.

The Dodger heaves himself up and slowly follows him through the warehouse and out the small door they entered through.

When he gets outside, the sun is low in the sky, and the bodyguard has disappeared.

CHAPTER 23

Frankie

It's getting darker. Night will come soon. I wonder if I'll be able to sleep. Now I know it wasn't Danilo chasing me in New Orleans, but somebody was. And it had to be one of the crew. Who else would chase me all over the city from the French Quarter and follow my streetcar through all the streets with the foreign names until I got off?

So, I've been standing here at the rail ever since the last crate was loaded, watching the off-watch crew returning to *Il Destino* after their day of shore leave. Papa told me that many of them buy presents in each port for their families back home. I wonder what they bought here? Not the beignets I never got to try; they'd go stale. Maybe jazz records everybody talks about?

I count seventeen of them so far—four officers and thirteen unlicensed seamen. I recognize them all even if I still haven't learned all their names, like the bow-legged man with the fuzzy hair and the pock-marked face. He's a steward and a friend of Danilo's. Could he have been the one following me?

Next to him is Malik, from Senegal, who works in the engine room. Could Malik have been the one?

Oh, I'm wasting my time even thinking about it.

At least I can eliminate half the crew, the half that went on shore leave yesterday and had to stay aboard *Il Destino* today. So, it can't be my friend Winston. I can cross him off my list of suspects, along with all the others who aren't returning to the ship now. Edvard, Osvaldo, Magnus, and Drago were on shore leave today, but I'd hate to think it was one of them. First Mate Garafolo was, too. If it has to be anyone, I want it to be him. None of them has boarded yet. If they don't get here soon, I think they will be considered AWOL, or whatever the Merchant Marine word is for that.

The sun hits my left eye on a slant. Soon, it's going to dip below the horizon, and it will be dark. I want to be back in my cabin when that happens. If one of the men boarding the ship now was the one chasing me in New Orleans, it wouldn't be too hard for him to knock me out and toss me overboard while everyone else is busy.

I look at them all again as they climb the gangway. It has to be one of them, but which one?

CHAPTER 24

Frankie

The day is sunny and breezy but warmer than yesterday. Maybe this is a good sign after the bad things that have happened since before we left Baltimore. The Wiper being murdered. My running away and hiding in a warehouse. Someone chasing me in New Orleans.

My father stands at the top of the gangway, greeting the six passengers who will be traveling across the Atlantic with us. The first on is a couple about the same age as my mom's parents. He's tall and thin; she's shorter than I am and looks happy to be here.

My father shakes their hands and introduces them to First Mate Garafolo, who also shakes their hands. He takes them to the purser, who checks their passports and the yellow card in them. I have a yellow card in my passport, too; I got it last year when Mom and I flew to Italy. It shows that I've been vaccinated for a bunch of diseases. The first mate guides them to the rail near the ship's bow. Another couple of about the same age arrives right behind them. This time, it's the woman who is tall and thin. The husband is almost a head shorter than she is and wider than his wife. After my father greets them and the purser does the same passport check, Second Mate Nunziamo takes them over to the first couple, who are still talking to the first mate.

The next passenger is a man dressed in a suit and vest like he's on the way to his office. He's younger than the others, maybe younger than my father, and he doesn't seem to be very happy to be going on a cruise.

Unlike him, the lady behind him, the last one to board, looks excited. As warm as it is, she's wrapped in a mink coat. She's short, with tiny bird bones. Her smile is so wide, I could probably count her teeth if I tried. They're very white, and her lipstick is bright red, like in a technicolor movie. I didn't think it was possible, but when she sees my father, her smile gets even wider. When he offers her his hand to shake, she takes it in both of hers like he's an old friend she hasn't seen in years. It's hard to figure out her age, but she looks very pleased when my father leads her and the sad-looking man over to the other four passengers.

Il Destino is the first of the Vittoria Lines' ships to take on passengers. It's lucrative, Danilo says, with each passenger paying as much as a $130 a day for the pleasure of being on a cargo ship.

He can't understand why they would pay as much money as it would cost to travel in more luxury, and more quickly, on ocean liners like the *United States* or the *Leonardo da Vinci*. But my father says other cargo ships have been carrying passengers for years now because some people like the adventure of not knowing how long they will be in each port—or even which ports they visit. Danilo says the company directors place great trust in my father and his abilities and tact, which is why they picked his ship as the first to be outfitted for passengers.

I know how my father feels about my being here on a normal voyage, his worries about my not getting the right schooling, and about the dangers of being surrounded by all these men. Now he's worried about how I will act with these six people, four of them old enough to be retired, and how they will react to me—so much so, that he's asked me to stay out of their way. He and the other officers will be dining with them each evening, but I will have dinner alone in the officers' mess. I don't know what he thinks I would do to upset them. Spill food down my blouse? Burp at the table? Tell corny jokes? In his mind, I'm about six years old.

I wish he trusted me more, like Mom always did.

CHAPTER 25

Frankie

I'm standing in front of the blackboard with the heading, *Sounding with oil.* Under it on the left, it says *Bailout date* and on the right *Cargo Comp,* with a lot of fill-in-the-blanks kind of lines. It's our first full day at sea since leaving New Orleans.

"What are you doing here?"

I stop myself from screaming. First Mate Garafolo does stuff like that—sneaking up on me and yelling in my ear. That's one of the reasons I don't like him.

And he sure doesn't like me. In fact, he might even hate me. Danilo says I have to stay on the first mate's good side. He calls him Garafolo when the first mate is not around. Danilo says Garafolo can get my father in trouble, so I have to be extra careful not to do anything Garafolo can use against him.

"I was just wondering what those words meant and these numbers here." I point to the list below the headings that has lines next to it filled in with numbers in chalk. I smile at him the way I used to smile at Mrs. Morris in Algebra class when she caught me letting Ellen copy my homework. It always worked with Mrs. Morris, but it's not working with the first mate.

"You don't belong here."

I know what he means. He means that I don't belong on *Il Destino.* But before he can start his usual lecture about children and females and bad luck, I interrupt him.

"You're right, Mr. Garafolo. I don't belong here." From the look on his face, I can tell I surprised him. Then, I add, "I should be back in my cabin doing my Geography lesson. I'd better run." And I start to leave, but he blocks the door.

So, here I stand, helpless, as he accuses me of being responsible for, among other things, the fact that there might be a killer on board. By his reasoning, if my father had not decided to bring me onto the ship, the Wiper would still be alive, even though he died before I boarded; the gale we encountered four days ago would not have occurred; and the second mate would not have come down with food poisoning from the lunch he ate at a café in the French Quarter.

All this after he accuses me of holding up our departure from port because I got lost. Never mind that the cargo was loaded on time, the passengers didn't board until the next day, and the ship left on schedule.

I keep my arms rigidly at my sides. This is so hard for me. If anyone had shouted at me like this in Baltimore—the school principal, Aunt Bess, even—I would have turned and walked away without saying a word. But I can't do that with the first mate, for my father's sake. So, I don't move and keep an unreadable expression on my face as he hollers at me. I'm sure he has no idea what I'm feeling. He can't tell if I'm afraid of him, or embarrassed and humiliated. I make sure there's no way he can, which makes him even angrier.

I already apologized to him for "any trouble I caused," and haven't said a word since. He hasn't given me a chance.

Then, Danilo comes in.

"Francesca, would you like me to get your father?" The look on Garafolo's face tells me that Danilo will be the next in line to receive the same treatment I've been getting. The first mate dismisses me as if I were an unlicensed seaman and turns to Danilo. I know it's not the first time Danilo has had to take a verbal beating from him. He's told me that everyone on the ship except my father has to put up with the man's temper.

I start to leave. At the door, I look back. Danilo is standing there, his arms rigidly at his sides—the same posture I used.

CHAPTER 26

The Dodger

So, the captain's daughter made it back to the ship. The Dodger still doesn't understand why she ran out of that shop, why she jumped onto that streetcar, or why she started running again when she got off at the other end.

His guess is that she thought someone was after her. But from the shy smile she just gave him, it's clear that she doesn't know it was him. Therefore, there's no reason why his back-up plan won't still work—except that *Il Destino* will be at sea and he would have to hold her and hide her on the ship. And keep her hidden until the ship reaches Naples.

The Dodger knows he must do everything to avoid that because it's so risky. He must try to solve this puzzle of the document's location by using his brains. He tells himself that he's clever enough to do that, to figure out where the Wiper hid it. He just needs to put himself into the Wiper's head. It shouldn't be too difficult. They share a country and a language. They share the same background. They just don't—or in the Wiper's case, didn't—share a political ideology. The Wiper was one of those democracy-is-everything people.

The problem is time. The ship will reach Naples in less than twelve days. It's a big ship, and even in his off-hours, the Dodger won't have time to search everywhere the document might be. So, he must use his brains and think. If he were the Wiper and wanted to hide something on a cargo ship so it wouldn't be found, where would he hide it? The Wiper was smart—not smart enough to avoid getting killed, but smart enough to know that he couldn't hide the document near where he slept.

The Dodger decides to do what he realizes he should have done in the beginning, walk the ship, carefully so no one wonders what he's up to, and note every possible hiding place. If someone is around, he will return when it is safe to search. He knows it would be easier if he really did have the sailing experience his papers said he had when he signed on. Then, he could have looked at those possible hiding places his first few days on board. A ship this size must have many.

He's off duty. It's not raining, and the sea is calm. He will start with the deck.

He begins at the forecastle and works his way aft. He ignores the cargo hatches. These have been opened in both ports, Baltimore and New Orleans, and, as he loaded and unloaded each cargo at each port, he feels like he has searched every one of the many possible hiding places in each. If the Wiper hid the document in any of them, the Dodger would have been found it by now. He ignores the windlass, as well. The Wiper would have had to take it apart to hide the document inside. The Dodger doesn't think it would be possible to do quickly and certainly not possible to do with no one noticing. And the document would probably have been so damaged that it would have been of no use to the Wiper and his fellow democracy fanatics.

One of the ventilators? The Wiper would have had to really secure the document so it stayed in place and wasn't blown out. The Dodger will eliminate the ventilators for now.

Does the fact that the Wiper worked there rule out the engine room even though he would never be alone there? No, just the opposite. The Wiper would have to be there as part of his job, and he wouldn't always be under the eye of one of the engineers or the electrician or the oiler. It would be easy for him to hide the document there and retrieve it later.

But not easy for the Dodger. He can't think of a single reason why he would be there—not a reason that the engineers or the others would believe. The only reason is one he can't tell them—that he needs to find an incriminating document which could topple the new government of his country. So, for now, the engine room is off limits.

There's another reason he's putting off a search there. When he first signed on, he'd never been below deck on a ship before. The captain and chief mate didn't know that, of course; his forged certificate said otherwise. It said that he had an entry-level rating. The only time he had been required to go to the engine room was his first day on board. He was thankful then that he wasn't one of the crew there. The noise and the lack of sunlight brought back too many memories, ones he hadn't permitted himself to think about since the war. The engine room was too much like the cellar in Paris where he aided the Obersturmbannführer in his interrogations. The engine room is hot, not cold like the cellar. And the noise comes from machines, not humans. But there is something there, something that brought it all back, something that made it hard for him to breathe. If he believed in a god, he would pray that he would find the document before he has to search the engine room. But he doesn't, so he will just hope.

Besides, he can't figure out how and when to search it since it's never been left empty in all the time he's been on this ship. But one thing he learned in the last couple of weeks is that the engineering crew deals with more than the ship's engines. They deal with the lighting and water systems, even the sewage. Not all their work takes place in the bowels of the ship. The document does not have to be in the engine room. It could be anywhere the Wiper could be without raising suspicion.

There is equipment in the galley, for instance, that would need the attention of the engineering department. The galley, with its refrigerators and ovens and stoves. Would a Wiper work on galley equipment? Maybe yes, maybe no. He can't ask anyone because, as an experienced seaman, he's supposed to know. But he doesn't.

CHAPTER 27

Frankie

I'm in the lounge with two of the passengers today. The lounge is very fancy because the shipping line redecorated it before *Il Destino* sailed from Italy. The sofas and chairs are made of smooth, red velvet, which is a nice change from the gray of the rest of the ship. I love to sit on the sofa because I sort of sink down. It's like being wrapped up in a warm, soft blanket. There are dark wood coffee tables and matching end tables. The passengers put their drink glasses right on them without using a coaster. Aunt Bess would just die!

There's a black, shiny bar with a greenish light running around it just below the top. Before the passengers came on board, I used to sit on one of the stools and pretend I was ordering a cocktail. Now, Danilo or one of his men stands behind the bar and makes the passengers real cocktails.

My father says I should avoid all the passengers during the voyage, which I've tried to do. But they haven't avoided me. They've all been really friendly, so when Mrs. Church asked me to have a cup of tea with her and Mr. Church, and I told her I wasn't allowed to do that, she said, "Nonsense," and Mr. Church said, "Ridiculous. Of course, you can have tea with us. I'll square it with your father."

What could I do? I can't upset the passengers by saying no. I don't want to, anyway. I feel like I haven't talked to anyone in years. My father and Danilo have been so busy since we left New Orleans and so has Drago. I have talked to Magnus, Edvard, Osvaldo, and Winston, but only when they had to tell me something

Now here I am talking with Mrs. Church—another female. The first mate probably hates that.

"Have another cookie, Francesca." Mrs. Church insists on calling me Francesca instead of Frankie because she says it's one of the most beautiful names she's ever heard. When she said that, it reminded me of my mother because she said the same thing. So, Francesca it is.

As I chew my cookie, Mrs. Church tells me all about her granddaughter, Robin, who is two years older than me and ready for college.

"You remind me so much of her, you know. She's very pretty, bright, too, and has good manners, just like you." I wish my father was hearing this.

Mr. Church nods but doesn't say anything. He doesn't seem to get much of a chance to talk when he's around his wife. I like them both. They're nothing like my Baltimore grandparents. Mrs. Church is nice and round. She still has a lap that I'm sure Robin was comfortable sitting on when she was little. As she hands me the plate and I take another cookie, Mrs. Church asks what I do all day since I'm not in school and my friends aren't around.

I swallow what's in my mouth and answer. "Well, I eat breakfast early, usually with my father; then I do my school work; then I eat lunch; then I take a *pausa*—that's a sort of recess—to get some exercise. After that, I finish my school work, then have dinner in the officers' mess. Afterwards, if he's not busy, my father goes over my work with me. When we're finished, I go back to my cabin and do my homework and go to bed." I reach for another cookie.

"That's a lot of school work. I'm impressed," Mr. Church says, between sips of his cocktail. And he looks impressed.

"Do you ever get to read anything that isn't school related?" Mrs. Church asks.

"Well, the problem is that when I packed to leave with my father, I didn't have a lot of time. I remembered to bring my textbooks but didn't have a chance to pack any other books."

"Like Nancy Drew?"

"Oh, I liked those mysteries a lot. I read all of them a long time ago."

"So, you like mysteries?" I nod because my mouth is full of cookie crumbs. "So does Robin. Have you ever read anything by Agatha Christie?" My mouth is still full, so I shake my head. "I think you'd enjoy her books; Robin does. Here, take this one." She picks up her handbag from the floor next to her and fishes around in it—it's very big—and finally brings out a hardback book with a red cover and a tombstone on it. "I just finished it. If you like it, I have some more I've already read that you can have. I was going to leave them on the ship for the next group of passengers, anyway. Maybe when you're finished reading them, you can start a little library here."

I swallow the last cookie bite. "That's a great idea. I bet my father will like that." She really is a very nice lady. I take the book from her and open it, then remember my manners. "Thank you so much, Mrs. Church. I'm sure I'll love it."

And maybe I'll get some ideas from it about how to solve my own real-life mystery.

CHAPTER 28

The Dodger

The galley is warm from the day-long meal preparations. It smells of hot cooking oil and warm bread and fried onions. Most important, it's empty. Besides the noise of the sea and the ship moving through it, the only sound is the hum of the refrigerators. The Dodger decides that it should be safe to search it.

He starts at the ceiling and works his way downward, checking every cabinet, underneath every space that has an underneath, in, as well as under and behind, every drawer. The cabinets are crammed with containers of oil, lard, flour, and other food, along with cooking equipment. Everything is orderly and seems to be where it's supposed to be. There is no place to hide the document where it wouldn't be found by one of the mess men. He goes back to the ceiling and starts to remove the covers of the overhead lights, then realizes that the document would probably have caught fire if it had been hidden there. The same with the oven.

The only places left are the refrigerators. He opens one, pulls out the containers in the front, and places them on the floor to check the back.

He is pulling open the bins at the bottom of the first refrigerator when he hears footsteps. He presses himself against the wall on the galley side of the mess.

There's not enough time to put the containers back. It would be too noisy; so would shutting the refrigerator door. If whoever is there walks in, how does he explain this? His mind freezes; he can't think of a single reason why he should be here and, especially, why the refrigerator contents are scattered on the floor. He hears whoever it is shuffling around in the mess. If it's food he's after, he'll come in here to get it. Can the Dodger knock him out before he sees him? He will have to.

The Dodger waits. He hears no movement on the other side. He pulls himself as close as possible to the wall, his hands pressed against it on either side of his hips. Seconds, maybe minutes, go by. If whoever is in the mess is making any noise, it's being drowned out by the sounds of the sea outside and the galley refrigerators. The Dodger's hands are shaking, and he clenches them in anger.

He pushes himself from the wall and prepares to confront whoever is on the other side. But as he steps into the mess, whoever it is steps into the companionway, his back to the Dodger. The Dodger waits a minute to make sure he doesn't come back, then returns to the galley to replace the containers in the refrigerator as quickly as possible.

Too quickly. The one containing something red packed in liquid slips from his hands and breaks into a thousand shards. Did whoever just left the galley hear the crash? The Dodger pushes himself against the wall again and waits. If he heard, how long before the seaman would return? The Dodger waits and waits some more. Finally, he realizes the seaman won't be returning. Someone else might, though. He runs out of the galley, then out of the mess.

Somebody else can take the blame for the broken container. It won't be him.

CHAPTER 29

Frankie

My father is sitting at his desk, and Danilo is standing next to him. I was about to go in and ask about a Geometry problem I'm having trouble with, but I decide to stay in the companionway and listen, just in case they say something interesting. Lately, I've learned a lot by listening when no one knows I'm there.

My father closes the log and sits back in his chair, rubbing his eyes and yawning at the same time.

"You're tired, Captain. Can I get you some coffee?"

"No, thank you, Danilo. Coffee wouldn't do any good right now." He looks around and up at him. "You're getting married in the autumn, aren't you?"

"Yes, Captain."

"And you're planning on having children?"

Danilo seems surprised at the question.

"Of course, Captain, as many as God sends us."

"How will you manage being a father when you'll be at sea most of the year?" The way he asks this question, I know he's wondering how he'll manage as my father. I want to tell him that he's managing fine, but then I wouldn't hear what comes next. It might be something I need to know.

"Our families will help my wife. My parents. Her parents," Danilo explains.

"Ah, *la famiglia*. My Francesca doesn't have a helping family. Only me." His voice drops as he says this.

"She's a good girl, Captain."

"Yes, she's a good girl. An enthusiastic girl. She gets that from her mother. And impetuous. She gets that from her mother, too. How my wife came from a family like hers, I don't know."

I've often wondered that myself.

"And they don't want Francesca?"

My father nods.

"And your own family, Captain?"

"There's no one. My father hasn't spoken to me in years, not since I chose the sea instead of the family ranch."

"There's a family ranch?"

This is a surprise. Mom never told me.

"Yes. A cattle ranch. It's big and successful, and any son would be happy and grateful to inherit it.' Those are my father's words, not mine. But it wasn't the life I wanted. I've always wanted to be at sea. I knew that since my parents first took me to Talamone when I was eight years old. But my father never understood."

"What about your mother? Does she understand?" Danilo asks him exactly what I want to know.

"She did, but she died shortly after I left the ranch. That's another reason my father won't talk to me. He blames my leaving for her death."

"But he would talk to his own granddaughter, wouldn't he?"

"Perhaps, Danilo, perhaps. A disobedient son is one thing, but a granddaughter? Even if he would welcome her, I don't know if it would be much better than her situation here. According to my cousin, my father is living on his own, with only a housekeeper who comes in each day to clean and cook. Taking care of a boy would be hard enough for him. But a girl? A girl needs a woman's care. Someone to talk to her, to teach her to cook. Someone she can talk to about personal things. My father can't do that. Still, it would give her some stability, instead of constantly going from port to port."

Does that mean that he might send me to live with this grandfather I've never met when we dock in Naples? If there's still a killer on board, he might.

We'll reach Naples in five days, so I've got to find the killer before then, or I might end up on a cattle ranch with a man I've never met. I don't know if I can do this alone. And there's only one person I can trust to help me.

My father's hands move from rubbing his eyes to rubbing his scalp. As he does this, he looks at the photo of our family on his desk. The Three Bears picture. Just the three of us.

Now, just the two of us.

CHAPTER 30

The Dodger

He spends the next day working and asking himself where else the document could be. The engineering crew takes care of the lifeboats, but they were inspected before the passengers boarded. The document would have been found, and the whole crew questioned.

It can't be the water systems. Even in a water-proof bag, the Wiper would never chance the document being damaged or destroyed. Then it would be of no value to him in his efforts to smear the name of the Leader.

The lighting? Every compartment on the ship has lighting of one sort or the other that the engine crew is responsible for. But the Dodger dismisses that possibility for the same reason he dismissed the lights in the galley. The heat could easily damage the document, and could, in fact, start a fire. The air conditioning systems wouldn't work for the same reason.

In one of the cargo containers? No. The containers that were on the ship when the Wiper was alive have been off-loaded. Those on the ship now were loaded after the Dodger killed him.

The lounge? The saloon? Would the Wiper have taken a chance on being spotted in either place? There would be no reason for him to be there, but if he was desperate?

Another possibility is in the swimming pool the company had installed when they decided to take on passengers. It hasn't been filled with water yet—it will be months before it is—but it does have a cover on it, so the Wiper could have taped the document to the side of the pool and no one would know.

But anyone in the wheelhouse could have looked down any second and seen the Wiper doing that. Could the Wiper have hidden it in the pool without detection? Maybe when the ship was in port? The Dodger decides he will have to wait until the ship reaches Naples. It will have to be the very last place he looks.

He passes the funnel. Then the purser's office, which is always locked if the purser isn't there. The Wiper couldn't hide the document there; he wouldn't be able to access it. The only places left are the saloon, the lounge, the infirmary, the docking bridge, and the engine room. The Wiper would have had to take a big chance of being caught in the saloon or the lounge. The Dodger will have to take that same chance. Because of the medicines stored there, the infirmary is usually locked, but the Wiper could have pretended he was ill and hidden it there. Though it's difficult to gain access to it, the Dodger knows he will need to check there at some point.

The Dodger decides that he needs to go back to the engine room crew's quarters. The document wasn't under the Wiper's mattress or any of the others or in their lockers, but he could have hidden it inside his mattress or even inside the mattress of one of the other crew. If it's not there or in the saloon or lounge, only then will the Dodger need to find a way to search the infirmary, swimming pool, and engine room.

Seven bells struck at least twenty minutes ago. If the Dodger isn't careful, he'll be late.

CHAPTER 31

Frankie

Danilo and I are in the lounge, empty now of the passengers, who have all returned to their cabins to change for dinner. I'm sitting in the middle of the deep-red sofa, my body barely making an impression on the thick, velvet cushions. Danilo's in one of the matching chairs on the other side of the coffee table, explaining in more detail why he took me to that creepy shop in the French Quarter.

"I knew you were hungry. I'm sorry I didn't pay any attention. All I could think of was Lilianna and why there were no letters from her. She has complained—many times—about my being away so many months of the year. When I am there, at home, I can convince her that it's worth it, that I can make much more money and take better care of her if I work on a ship."

"You don't need to apologize. I understand." But he continues as if I hadn't said a thing.

"Lilianna is beautiful, and many men want to marry her. So, when there were no letters waiting for me in New York, then none in Baltimore or New Orleans, I thought that one of those men had won her away from me. I had to know if she was still mine. I had to call her. Her family doesn't have a telephone, so I needed to call the fire station next door to her house and one of the firemen had to go and get her. By the time she got to the phone and told me everything was fine and that she'd written but the letters hadn't caught up with me, almost twenty-five minutes had passed." He leans back in his chair. "I should have known that she'd written me. Many times, letters to the crew never reach us. If the home office doesn't get them to the port agent in time, we won't see them until our next trip to that port and maybe not even then." He spreads his hands out in a there-you-are-that's-the-whole-story gesture.

"It's okay, Danilo. All that's over. We have more important things to talk about."

"We do?"

"Yes. We need to talk about catching the Wiper's killer. He has to be on the ship. We have to figure out who it is or at least why he killed the Wiper. Because if we know why, we might be able to figure out who. So, the first thing I need is for you to tell me about the Wiper. Where was he from? What was he like?"

"It doesn't matter where he was from or what he was like. You need to stop this."

"Please, Danilo, just tell me."

"There's nothing for me to tell. He only joined the crew in New York. I never talked to him, so I have no idea what he was like."

"But you must know where he was from."

Danilo shakes his head. "He could have been from anywhere, but probably Europe somewhere."

That's not very helpful. Half the crew are from Europe somewhere. I have more questions, but Danilo stops me.

"Frankie, finding the killer is something for the police in Baltimore to do, not you."

"How can they do that back there? They said the killer's still here, in the middle of the Atlantic. My father knows this, and he'll fret about it every minute, so by the time we reach Naples, he'll definitely think I should live on land and not on the ship." I'm leaning forward, my elbows on my knees and looking him directly in the eyes. "That means that we have to find the killer; then Papa can arrest him and give him to the Italian police. Maybe they'll give him to the Baltimore police. I don't care who gets him. The ship will be safe again, and Papa will stop worrying about me."

Danilo shakes his head and stands up like he's about to go and tell Papa about my plan. I should have sworn him to secrecy before I said anything. I jump up from the sofa before he can move a step.

"You can't tell him, Danilo. If he knows, he'll put me on a plane to Baltimore as soon as we dock in Naples. I can't go back there; they don't want me. I can't leave my father. Please. Please don't tell him." I have my hands pressed together like I'm praying. What I'm really doing is begging.

He sits down again, so I do, too.

He leans forward and takes my hand. "He can't send you back there, Frankie. I don't know how, but your uncle found out about your running away and hiding in the warehouse. When your father called him in New Orleans, your uncle said that since your behavior hasn't changed, he felt it's best that you don't return to them."

I know how Uncle Ronnie found out. He has contacts in the police. One of them, maybe even the Commissioner himself, would have told him. Then Aunt Bess probably found out, and it was just the excuse she needed. It's a relief to know this, but it doesn't solve my present problem.

"Danilo, I know about my grandfather, the one in Italy, I mean. I know I have one and that my father might send me to live with him. I don't know him—I didn't even know he was alive—and if he won't talk to his own son, I don't want to meet him. But if we don't find the killer by the time we reach Naples, I might have to live with him."

"Where?"

"Danilo! Aren't you listening? With Papa's father. My grandfather. In Sinalunga. For all I know, he might be worse than my mother's father."

"No, no, Frankie."

"Yes, yes, Danilo. He could be."

"But the captain's father won't talk to him. So, how can the captain take you there? No, Frankie. You have to stay on the ship. Where else can you go?"

Where else can I go? To my mom's parents, who not only don't like me; they don't like my cousins either? To another boarding school?

Some days I miss my mom more than others. This is one of those days.

I'm trying not to cry, but it doesn't work. I can feel my cheeks getting wet. I swipe my sleeve across my face and apologize. Danilo pulls a handkerchief out of his pocket and hands it to me. As I blow my nose into it, he leans forward.

"I won't tell your father, Frankie. Not now, anyway."

I nod. I think it's my crying and not my begging that changed his mind. I'll have to remember that. But I can't let our conversation end there. I've got to convince him to help me find the killer.

"But you do understand why I have to do this, Danilo, don't you?"

"I understand why you *think* you have to. You think this will be easy. But I know it could be dangerous."

"Look at it this way. It will be less dangerous than having a killer roaming all over the ship."

Danilo can't argue with this. Not because he agrees; I can see he doesn't. He can't argue because he hears the passengers heading this way. He jumps up and takes his place behind the bar.

The Manuccis are the first to arrive. Mr. Manucci points at me.

"Danilo, please fix this young lady a Shirley Temple cocktail." Mr. Manucci sits down at the bar and pats the stool next to him. I hop onto it and lean my elbows on the bar. He does the same and winks.

"Just two pals having a drink together," he laughs.

Danilo does what he says, but as he hands me my drink, his eyebrows are drawn down close to his eyes. I'd think he was just squinting if I didn't know his expressions so well by now. This expression means he's having doubts about something—probably about the promise he just made me.

CHAPTER 32

The Dodger

The ship is rolling, swaying from side to side. The Dodger bites down on the seasickness that threatens to overwhelm him. He has no time to waste on vomiting. The ship will reach Naples in four days and every nautical mile that brings *Il Destino* closer to it means less time to find the document.

The quarters that the engine room crew share are empty and dark, but the Dodger doesn't turn on the light. There's always the chance that one of the crew will return, and the Dodger might have to knock out whoever it is before he's recognized. That's if the Dodger can hear him over the wailing of the storm outside.

The radiator is on full blast. He pulls out his handkerchief and wipes his forehead, chin, and neck. He unclips his Marlin Spike from his lanyard and heaves the first of the four thin mattresses onto its side. This is where the Wiper slept; he found out. The spike slides easily through the top seam on the side of the mattress.

CHAPTER 33

Frankie

The rain is coming down so hard that the noise of it hitting the deck drowns out the noise of the wind. According to Danilo, it's a Nor'easter and I need to stay below deck or in my cabin.

I am bored, bored, bored. I've finished all my studying and all my homework. The passengers are in their cabins, so there's no one to talk to. And I can't read, or I'll get seasick because the words on the pages keep moving. I decide to do my own deck walk but below deck instead of on it. I haven't really explored some parts of the ship.

My cabin is on the port side, where the passengers stay. The engine room crew's quarters are on the starboard side. The chief engineer gave me a tour of the engine room, which I thought was loud, hot, and not a place I'd want to work. I won't go there today because just to get there, you have to go backwards down what the crew calls 'stairs' and anybody else would call a 'ladder.'

It's no use going to the lounge or saloon. They're only interesting when the passengers are there. So, I decide to go to the back of the ship, aft. I climb down to the No. 2 'tween deck, through the hatch and past the fridge lockers, up to the No. 3 center-castle and past the saloon and the unlicensed seamen's mess and main galley, then down another set of stairs—carefully because the ship is rolling from side to side—to another companionway, which is narrow enough that I can put my hands on both wall sides to keep upright. It's hard enough to walk straight from the bow to the aft on the deck. It's impossible to stay on one level when you're going from one end of *Il Destino* to the other below deck.

I reach the area where the engine room crew sleep. some of them are probably sleeping now, so I try to be quiet. Even though the sound of the waves beating against the side of the ship would drown out any noise I make, I tiptoe anyway. This isn't easy when the ship keeps moving, and I need to keep moving myself so I don't get sick. Also, I'm wearing those saddle shoes my aunt bought me after I grew out of the last sneakers and loafers Mom had bought for me. Well, Aunt Bess said I grew out of them; I thought they fit fine. That's one thing I'm going to get my father to buy me when we reach Naples, a pair of sneakers. If they sell sneakers there.

I tiptoe past the crew's quarters but then turn back to look through the door. It's dim and shadowy inside, but I can see the silhouette of a man sitting on the metal edge of a bunk, twisted so that his back is toward me. I can recognize everyone on the ship now, but it's too dark to see who he is. I guess I could say hi, just to have someone to talk to.

I decide not to. I don't know why. There was just something, I don't know, something a little spooky about him. He has a mattress pushed up on its side and a short knife like the one my father owns in his hand. Probably not a good idea to talk to a man with a knife in his hand—unless he's a cook, of course, or a butcher like the man who rescued me in New Orleans.

Now, he's standing up with his back to me. It looks like he has his hand inside the mattress and is moving it back and forth and then farther inside. I can't figure out what he's doing, but whatever it is, I'm pretty sure it's not part of his job.

He pulls his hand out, throws the mattress back on the bunk and repeats the whole process with another one. Then he says something I can't catch because of the noise and throws that mattress on the floor. Maybe he's going to kick it and maybe, because he's so mad, "I'd best get out of here," as the butcher would say. I turn around. Even though I'm still on tiptoes and I'm not supposed to run, I take off down the companionway. Before I turn the corner, I look back.

He's not there. He hasn't seen me.

I don't stop running, though, not until I reach my cabin. As soon as I'm inside, I lock the door. I've never done that before.

Now I feel a little silly, acting like a frightened kid. I'm shaking, like I just woke up from a nightmare. But it was weird seeing a man cut up a mattress. Why would he do that?

I sink onto my bunk and try to catch my breath. That's when Aunt Bess pops into my mind again. Is she going to follow me everywhere? This time, it's, *Whatever has gotten into you, Young Lady?*

That's a good question, even if it does come from her. What has gotten into me? Why did I run? I mean, I know my father wouldn't like it if he thought I was "fraternizing" (he's actually used that word) with an unlicensed seaman, but that shouldn't make me run.

I get up and walk to the port hole. I love this view, all ocean, no buildings, no people, and, usually, no other ships. But I can't look out of it for long because the view is changing every second with the ship's movements. So, I walk back to my bunk and lie down. Maybe looking at the ceiling will help me figure out *why* I ran.

Then it hit me! The man cutting the mattress, he could be the Wiper's killer. After all, he had a knife. Was the Wiper killed with a knife? Danilo might know. In the gloom, I couldn't make out the color of his hair or even what he was wearing. All I could tell for sure is that he was tall.

So, the obvious question is: Who on the ship is that tall? Osvaldo and Winston are, and Edvard and Magnus. The only other ones that are tall are Garafolo and Drago, the third mate. They're officers, but there's no reason why an officer can't be a killer.

It can't be Winston. Not only was he not in New Orleans the day I was followed, I saw him cleaning up in the mess as I was passing there when I was headed to the engine room quarters. It would have been impossible for him to beat me down there. I'm glad; I like Winston a lot.

And the person I saw couldn't be Drago, either because he's on watch. But do I know that for sure? I don't. He probably could sneak away if he had to. So, he needs to stay on my list, along with the chief mate, Edvard, Magnus, and Osvaldo. It could be the chief mate. I mean, he's always mad at something and whoever was cutting open that mattress was definitely mad. I've never seen Osvaldo, Magnus, or Edvard act like that. They're always what Mom would call "easygoing."

Still, I can't eliminate them from my inquiries, as that police inspector in the Agatha Christie novel says. Being easygoing could be just an act. I need to find out where they all were when I saw the man cutting open the mattress. How can I do that? I can ask Danilo, but I have to be careful how I do it. He'll know why I want to know and give me another lecture on the dangers of finding a killer. And he might break his promise and tell Papa.

I'm going to have to think about this.

CHAPTER 34

Frankie

The gale is now throwing up forty knots-an-hour winds, and the Atlantic is so choppy that nothing on the ship seems to be standing still. It's the roughest it's been since I've been on board. Funny thing is that now I don't feel queasy at all, not like before. Danilo says that storms like this are common at sea, and all the crew are used to them. Looks like I'm getting used to them, too.

I head to the lounge, but the passengers still aren't there—only Danilo, and he looks worried. I jump onto a bar stool and order my usual, a Shirley Temple cocktail, and tell Danilo not to worry.

"They probably decided to skip their cocktail, so they don't become seasick. "

"I don't think so, Frankie. But we'll find out at dinner."

What we find out at dinner is that not a single passenger showed up to eat it. None of the officers were there, either, because they were all needed at their stations. Danilo is now sure that the passengers are all seasick. He is pacing back and forth in front of the table.

"It's okay, Danilo. It's not your fault they got sick."

"But nobody thought about this, nobody at the Home Office did. Your father didn't. I doubt the passengers did." He stops pacing and faces me. "I've got to check on them."

"I'll come with you."

When we go to their cabins to check that they are all right, we find that none of them are. Mr. Church opens the door to their cabin, then runs to the bathroom. We can hear him throwing up and decide we'd best leave him alone. Mrs. Church is lying scrunched up on her side, her eyes closed, and her hand holding onto the side of the bed. The Manuccis won't even let Danilo in.

Mr. Jerome does let Danilo come in, but only to beg him to make it stop. Danilo thinks he meant the storm; I think he meant his seasickness.

When he knocks on Mrs. Dillon's door, there's no answer, so he knocks again. When there's still no answer, he turns to me.

"Would you go in, Frankie? You're a female."

I find her lying on her stomach on her bunk, her head hanging over a trash can. When I ask if we can do anything, she answers by giving a little wave to send me away.

Danilo tells them all that he will bring some medicine called Valontan, which they carry on board. He's mumbling something as we leave the passenger area.

"What?"

He stops and looks right at me. "The problem is that you're supposed to take it *before* you get seasick, not after, so I don't know if it'll do any good. And we don't carry much of it. If I give it to them now, suppose we sail through another storm before we reach Naples, and we don't have any left? We should have given this more thought before we took on the passengers."

He turns around and jogs off, with me jogging right behind him. But instead of heading toward the infirmary, he turns in the direction of my father's quarters.

"I thought we were going to the infirmary to get the medicine."

"We are, but it's locked. I need to get the key from your father's office."

When we get there, Danilo goes to Papa's desk, opens the right, bottom drawer and takes out a ring with what looks like dozens of keys on it. Then, we're on our way to get the medicine that may or may not make the passengers feel better.

CHAPTER 35

Frankie

Now that the storm has passed, I can walk on deck again, and so can the passengers. The Valontan worked, at least for some of them. And none of them seem too upset about being sick At least, they haven't said anything about it. I really enjoy spending time with them, which surprised me because most of them are pretty old. They don't act old, though—definitely not as old as my grandparents do. Four of them are from Houston in Texas; the other two from Florida.

Of course, they don't know about there being a killer on board. That would be bad for business. Only three of us know about that—me, my father, and Danilo.

No, make that four. The killer knows. When I do figure out who he is, my father will have to arrest him in secret to keep it from the passengers. It had better happen soon, though, definitely before we reach Naples because the same crew is supposed to sail with us from there to the next port.

The passengers spend most of their time walking on the deck if the weather's okay; or in the lounge, reading and playing cards, and drinking tea or cocktails; or in the saloon eating. There's not a lot for them to do. It's too cold to play shuffleboard or swim even if the pool had water in it. So they don't die of boredom, my father has decided to hold a short lecture on Naples—its history, Mt. Vesuvis, Pompei and I don't know what else. Then, after we leave Naples, he'll arrange something similar for our next port of call. The problem is that he doesn't know what that port will be yet. He probably won't find out until we dock in Naples.

One of the passengers, Mrs. Church, is the one who gave me her book when she finished reading it. Turns out I really liked it, and when I told her, she gave me another one, also by Agatha Christie, but with a sleuth named Miss Marple. The cover on this one has a drawing of a woman holding her throat and looking like she's about to pass out. When I read it, I get an idea.

Suppose the killer and the Wiper knew each other before they started working on *Il Destino*? Suppose the reason the Wiper was murdered is because of something that happened before they got to Baltimore, before they even joined the ship? The murderer in the Agatha Christie book I just finished had met her victim a long time before she murdered her, and it was something that happened then, in the past when they first knew each other, that caused her to kill her victim many years later.

Or maybe the killer and the Wiper were friends and decided to sign on to the ship together and, once on board, had a fight at a bar near the port—a "falling out," as Agatha Christie would say—and the Wiper was killed during the fight. It might have been an accident, but the killer didn't give himself up because he thought he would be charged with murder and sent to prison.

I wonder where my father keeps the records of who joined the ship and when. In his logbook? I need to find out, but without him knowing. If he did find me looking at it, how could I explain it? I can't think what I could tell him. Plus, I don't know what he'll do. He might send me to a convent school that I couldn't escape from, or just as bad, to his father.

And I have to find the logbook without Danilo knowing. He already has doubts about me trying to find the Wiper's killer. If I'm not careful, he might tell my father what I'm up to. So, I'll wait until he's busy with the passengers and my father is on the bridge. No one will be in my father's office, so I can find the list of crew members and figure out where each one comes from. If two are from the same country, they might have known each other there. Maybe they grew up in the same neighborhood or went to school together. Maybe they were friends or even enemies. Like in the book, maybe the killer knew the Wiper before they came on board, and when he saw him again, decided to kill him because of some kind of revenge.

We'll be in Naples in less than four days. I need to get a look at that log as soon as possible.

CHAPTER 36

The Dodger

Now that the storm's over and everything's returned to normal, the Dodger resumes his search. Unless he finds it in the infirmary or lounge, he will not be able to avoid it any longer; he will have to search the engine room. But to search it without being seen, he would have to avoid the attention of at least two people, probably more. How to manage, that is the question he keeps asking himself. He could wait until there's only one seaman there and sneak down the ladder and behind some machines when the seaman is not looking. Risky. And is there ever a time when there is just one seaman there?

He waits until the middle of the night. There won't be many crew around at that hour. And the engine room does seem empty when he looks down the ladder, but the Dodger knows that's deceptive. The engine room is big and crowded with machines, and there's at least one person among them where he can't see him. The Dodger knows that he has to take the chance, though. He climbs down.

The smell of the diesel oil seeping up from the ship's hull makes him nauseous. Everything is metal and gray, with wheels sticking out at random. He has no idea what the machines are or what they do. Above him are pipes set at different angles, some so low that he has to duck to avoid hitting his head.

He doesn't get far before an engineer stops him.

"Lose your way?"

The Dodger looks at his watch. "Georgio asked me to meet him here," he tells the engineer and looks around as if he were lost. "At least, I think he said to meet him here. Or maybe the Radio Room?" The Dodger thickens his accent, hoping the engineer will think it's his bad English that's responsible for the mix-up. He does.

"Out," he roars. As the Dodger walks away, head bent to avoid hitting the overhead pipes, he bumps into a wheel jutting out of one of the gray mystery machines. He doesn't cry out with the pain or rub his hand on his thigh.

Behind him, the engineer adds, "And if you can't learn some English, try another ship. *Cretino*."

The Dodger has heard enough Italian to know what that means, but he doesn't look back.

The Dodger is lying in his narrow bunk, staring at the ceiling. The ship's now steady motion is tempting him to sleep, but he forces his eyes open. *Concentrate*, he tells himself.

Then, as he turns onto his other side, it comes to him. He knows how to empty the engine room, a simple way. So simple, he wonders why it took him so long to think of it. It will require gaining access to the infirmary, but he needs to search there anyway.

CHAPTER 37

Frankie

Each evening, the passengers eat their dinner in the saloon, then have after-dinner drinks and read or play Bridge in the lounge. When they finally return to their cabins, Danilo puts the lounge back in order, stacks the dirty glasses behind the bar for the mess man to pick up in the morning before breakfast, and writes a report for my father, a sort of log of what the passengers ate and didn't eat, drank and didn't drink, how much time they spent on deck, how much time in the lounge and in the bar, what they complained about and what they liked. This is not done on orders from the company; it's my father's idea. That way, the company can make adjustments on future voyages, not just on *Il Destino,* but on all its ships that will be carrying passengers. I'm sure that's another reason why he was promoted to captain at such a young age. He's smart.

Papa is on the bridge tonight, and all of these duties should keep Danilo busy enough for me to check the logbook in my father's office and copy the crew list, something Danilo probably wouldn't approve of but which is necessary to figure out who killed the Wiper. I'd better hurry, though, just in case.

The ocean is so calm after that storm that *Il Destino* seems as quiet as I ever remember it being since we left New Orleans. It's the same in my father's office, the only sounds the ticking of the wall clock and the rustle of the pages of the logbook as I turn them one by one. Actually, it's a little too quiet for me. I keep feeling like someone is silently tiptoeing up behind me.

Then I hear something that makes me jump halfway out of the chair. I whip my head around. No one's there. It's just the clock chiming the hour.

I hurry as much as possible. I want to get out of there before it chimes the quarter hour. I don't expect Danilo to show up here, but I don't know how long my father will be on the bridge.

"What are you doing?"

I jump again, this time all the way out of the chair, and drop the log onto my father's desk. "Oh. I didn't hear you." I smile at Danilo. He finished his duties earlier than I thought he would.

"What are you doing with the captain's log?" The overhead light is off. There's only the glow of the small reading lamp on the desk shining right on it.

"Nothing."

He doesn't change his expression. He just stands in the doorway—waiting.

"Oh, all right. I'm trying to find the list of crew members." I pick the log up again and shake it at him. "I can't find it in here anywhere. Do you know where my father keeps it?"

"He doesn't. The purser does. Why do you need the crew list?"

"Because I think I've found a way to figure out who the killer is."

"Frankie, you've got to stop this." He takes the log from me and puts it in the drawer where it belongs.

"Stop what?" I ask even though I know what he means.

"Stop trying to find the killer. It's dangerous, especially if whoever it is finds out what you're doing."

"See, you do think he exists." I cross my arms as I say this.

"Okay, I do. But don't you see, Frankie? That's even more reason for you to stop. This is someone who has killed another person, a human being. Do you think he wouldn't hurt you, even kill you, just because you're a girl? He would, Frankie, if he thought you were a danger to him. He would kill me, too, for the same reason."

"But you don't understand; I'll make sure that he doesn't know what we're up to. You don't have to worry."

"Yes, I do have to worry. Your father's right. It's too dangerous for you. The killer will find out—especially if you go snooping around like a policeman, like you're doing now."

"But Danilo—"

"No, Frankie. You have to stop this behavior. Right now. If you don't, I will have to tell your father, and you know what he'll do if he finds out."

I can tell he hates making this threat. He's felt sorry for me ever since Mom died. I really don't want to do this to him, but I have no alternative. I purse my lips, turn them down at the corners, and open my eyes wide so I look like I'm going to cry. It works; he takes back the threat.

"Don't cry, Frankie. I won't tell him. I promise. But you must stop this snooping around. You must be careful."

I grab his upper arms and give them a squeeze.

"Thank you, Danilo. I knew I could trust you." Then I run around him and out the door before he realizes that he's just made a big mistake. When he promised not to tell my father, he should have made me promise something, too—to stop trying to find the killer.

When I reach my cabin, the first thing I do is get down on my knees and pray. I haven't done this in a long time, not since Mom died and I got mad at God. But I really need God to do something for me. So, I pray really hard.

"Please, God," I say. "Please don't let Danilo go back on his promise and tell my father that he saw me looking through the log, and please let me stay with my father forever. Thank you, God. Amen."

There. All finished—English, Italian, History, Geography, and Geometry. In record time, too. Now, I can concentrate on how to catch a killer.

I haven't given up on my Agatha Christie idea. If I can find out which sailors are from the same country, I could maybe shorten my list of ones on shore leave that day in New Orleans. But I still have to get into the purser's office when no one's there, especially without Danilo catching me again. This time, I will have to be very, very careful.

To do that, I need to figure out when Danilo will be so busy with the passengers that he won't have time to come looking for me. Most important, I have to look when the purser isn't there. During dinner? He's an officer, so he eats with the passengers like the others. The trouble is, so do I. It will have to be the middle watch, then, when everybody except the crew on watch are sleeping in their bunks.

In the meantime, I'll start on the third Agatha Christie Mrs. Church gave me. I snuggle under the covers, prop the novel on my chest and turn to Chapter One. What murder will Hercule Poirot solve this time?

CHAPTER 38

Frankie

It's nearly 3:00 in the morning—six bells it's called on the ship—when I make my way along the companionway. I don't see anyone. That's good, but what if I run into trouble? There would be no one around to help me. But what trouble could I run into? The only danger would come from the killer, and why would he hurt me? He doesn't know I'm looking for him. How could he?

It's still too quiet for me, though, and now it's gloomy, too—and cold and damp like a graveyard after a heavy rain. An overhead light is out in the companionway, making it so dim that I have to watch where I'm walking. And I've never noticed before how creaky *Il Destino* is. I hope those sounds are coming because of the ship's motion and not because it's about to fall apart.

As I pass the steward's store, I feel a draft behind me, as if a hatch to the deck just opened. I whip around. There's no one there. No open hatch. No ghost. But there was definitely a draft; I'm sure of that. I let my breath out, turn back, and force myself to walk and not run. Finally, I pass the infirmary and reach the purser's office. I don't bother to knock or even peek in to see if someone's there. I just pull down the handle.

It's locked.

The purser is one of the officers who keeps away from me. He'll talk to me in the mess and when we have dinner with the passengers, probably to please my father, but he doesn't say much when he does. I don't know if he believes that silly superstition about females on board bringing bad luck or if he's just shy. Either way, he would never let me see the crew list. And he certainly wouldn't lend me the key to his office so I can look at it when he's not around. For one thing, he keeps money in there.

But his key can't be the only one on the ship. If he lost it, he'd have to break down the door to his own office and then leave it unlocked until it could be fixed. There's got to be a duplicate, and I bet I know where it is—on the ring of keys Danilo used to open the infirmary.

Is Papa a light sleeper? I'm his daughter; isn't that something I should know? It's important because if I'm going into his office in the middle of the night when he's right next door, he might wake up. I'll have to be super quiet.

I lied to my father only because I need to find the Wiper's killer. Now, I'm taking his keys for the same reason. Is it worth it? If he wakes up and catches me with the keys, what will he think? He would be disappointed in me. I can see the look he would give me, the why-did-you-do-that look like he did when I ran off to the warehouse. And angry, too, I bet. Angry enough to send me to a convent school? I know what I'm doing is wrong. But murder is even more wrong.

Only three days until we reach Naples. I have to see that list and see it now before I lose my nerve.

CHAPTER 39

The Dodger

Six bells. The other two deck hands he shares quarters with are snoring as usual. He waits a few minutes to make sure they aren't awakened by the bells. Then, he slips out of his bunk and out the door.

It's about as quiet as it gets on this tub. No storm raging outside. No officers yelling orders. No feet trodding heavily up and down the companionways. He might enjoy the quiet if he didn't have to steal something from right under the captain's nose.

On his way to the captain's quarters, he opens a hatch but sees something ahead. A shadow? A trick of the light? The lighting is so faint, it makes everything seem hazy. To be safe, he quickly closes the hatch and waits on the other side. If someone is there, he's probably on his way back to his bunk or to his duty station. Then he tells himself that it is probably what little glow there is shifting with the movement of the ship. And if there really was someone there, he's gone by now. The Dodger can't wait any longer; he needs to get in and out of the captain's office as soon as possible.

CHAPTER 40

Frankie

I move quickly toward my father's quarters since I'm not likely to run into anyone at this time of night. Still, I have to be careful. So, as I approach each corner, I stop and listen for footsteps or voices. No sound except the creaking of the ship.

Finally, I reach Papa's quarters. The door is unlocked. I slowly pull down the handle and open it, hoping it doesn't squeak. It doesn't. I tiptoe though the chart room to my father's office. The moon is three-quarters full and it isn't cloudy, so there's enough light coming through the porthole that I don't have to risk turning on a lamp. I inch up to my father's desk. He keeps the keys in the bottom, right drawer. Please don't let it be locked.

I squat down in front of the drawer and curl my fingers under the drawer pull. I stop for a moment. What if it squeaks and wakes my father? What do I do? If he did wake up, I'd probably hear him. Would I have enough time to run out of the office, down the companionway, and back to my cabin?

I pull the drawer open, slowly, slowly. No noise. But the keys? There are a lot of them on the ring; they might rattle when I move them. I close and open my hands, then wrap my right hand around the bunch. As quietly as possible, I scrunch them together and carefully lift them. Then, just as carefully, I close the drawer with my left hand and tiptoe out.

I make it back to the purser's office without being seen.

CHAPTER 41

The Dodger

The Dodger stops in front of the captain's quarters, puts his hand on the handle, ready to open it and hoping it's been properly oiled so it's silent. He looks right and then left. If something goes wrong here, there's no excuse that will keep him out of trouble. But he has no choice. He grabs the handle, pushes down, and opens the door.

There's enough moonlight pouring through the porthole that he doesn't need to use the flashlight he brought. He looks at the wall on each side of the chart room door, hoping that keys are hanging there. They're not there or next to the chalkboard. He enters the captain's office; the desk is on his left, the drawers facing him. If they're anywhere, he reckons, they would be in one of those drawers, unless he's really unlucky and the captain keeps them near where he sleeps.

He faces the desk and opens the narrow drawer above the kneehole. It's full of pencils, pens, paper clips, a ruler, all neatly in order. But no keys. He opens the top drawer on his left and finds two large black books with the shipping line's logo and the title *Captain's Log* in white. He checks the two drawers under that one. One contains stationery and envelopes, again with the shipping line's logo, and the other holds a large checkbook. The top two drawers on the right contain writing pads tidily stacked. He opens the bottom and last drawer. Empty.

He closes that drawer and looks around him. Where else could they be? Back in the chart room somewhere? If they're not there, he will have to give up his search for now. He dare not search the captain's cabin. He doubts that the captain would sleep through the Dodger searching inches away from him.

CHAPTER 42

Frankie

I have to try eight keys before I find the right one. I turn it in the lock and hear a click. I pull down the handle and open the door. Again, no squeak. I step inside, close the door, then stop. It's so dark I'm afraid to move and bump into something. I didn't think. I should have realized that there wouldn't be a porthole here.

I edge forward, my arm out in front of me, just like I did in the warehouse. Slowly, slowly. Tiny steps. My arm doesn't touch anything, but my leg does—a chair that rolls away and stops with a thud. Again, I put my arm out but lower until it hits cold metal. The desk.

There's got to be a lamp. Slowly, I feel around the surface of the desk until I find it. There's a chain. I pull it and the room lights up. I hope that no one can see the light from under the door.

There's another problem. I can't take the list with me. The purser is bound to notice it's missing. But I don't know how long it will take me to copy it. Suppose someone needs a key during that time and wakes my father to get it from him and my father finds out that the keys are missing? He might wake up the whole ship, and I'll be here instead of in my cabin.

There's only one thing to do. I've got to return my father's keys to his desk before I start copying the list. I take a deep breath, turn the lamp off, and feel for the door. When I leave, I pull the door partially shut, in case it locks automatically, and start back to my father's quarters.

Again, I'm lucky. I don't run into any seamen. I pass through the chart room and into my father's office and open the drawer. Holding the bunch in my hands just like I did when I took them out so they wouldn't rattle, I try to put the keys back where I found them in the same position they were in before. But my hand is shaking and when I start to put them down, they slip from my fingers and make a clattering noise.

I don't move. No sound from my father's cabin. I take a deep but silent breath. I can't wait any longer. So, hands still shaking, I arrange the keys like they were before, shut the desk drawer, and tiptoe out. I feel like yanking the door closed and running, but I don't. I shut it as slowly and silently as I did the first time.

CHAPTER 43

The Dodger

As he starts to slip into the chart room, the Dodger hears footsteps in the companionway. He just has time to hide behind the door before he hears someone walk quickly past and into the captain's office, the sound of a drawer opening, a slight clattering noise, and then the drawer closing.

Someone is returning the keys to the captain's desk. Who? The Dodger is fairly certain that whoever it is shouldn't be there. Quiet footsteps again coming closer. The door he's hiding behind starts to close. The Dodger waits a full minute before re-entering the captain's office.

When he reaches the infirmary, he spreads the keys out in his palm, then inspects the lock in front of him. It takes only two attempts before he's in.

First, his search for the document. Behind the desk and in it, behind and under each of its drawers. The same with the file cabinet. Nothing. Under the two beds and the mattresses. No time to cut them open but a quick look tells him the seams haven't been cut before. If the Wiper was a patient here, where else could he have hidden the document? The Dodger checks the cabinets that aren't locked. The Wiper wouldn't have access to the drugs that are in the locked cabinets. No, he didn't hide the document in the infirmary.

The Dodger grabs the bottle he needs from a closed door underneath the cabinets and shoves it in his pocket. He pulls the door to the infirmary closed behind him when he leaves and locks it. He puts the ring of keys in his other pocket, pulls his sweater down to hide the bulge they both make, and returns to the captain's quarters. Once inside, he slowly opens the right bottom drawer of the captain's desk. With the keys gripped tightly in his hand, he places them in the drawer and very quietly pushes it shut. After he squeezes out the door, he heads back to his berth.

Now, he has a good chance of getting into the engine room when no one's there.

CHAPTER 44

Frankie

It's still quiet in the companionway when I leave my father's quarters, but it seems darker. I look up at the lights on the ceiling, but nothing's changed. I hesitate. My cabin is so close; it would only take a minute for me to get there and slip inside. I look in its direction. No. I will not quit. I am a Moretti, and I will finish what I started.

Besides, I left the purser's door off the latch.

I put the list on the purser's desk, and I'm pulling out my pen to copy it when I hear a noise. I turn off the desk lamp, swivel the chair to face the door, and hold my breath. I hear it again, but can't make out what it is, only that it's not footsteps.

There it goes again. Is someone knocking on the door? I walk silently up to it and put my ear against it. This time, I can almost feel a thud right against the side of my face. I brace my shoulder against the door. The latch doesn't move. Then there's another noise, a scratching, like the sound a cat makes when it's trying to get you to let it go outside. I step back and move to the side. If whoever's on the other side breaks open the door, I will be hidden behind it. I try not to think about what will happen if that person closes the door, turns around, and sees me standing there.

I look around the purser's office. It's small, with just his desk, some file cabinets and a safe, all attached to the wall—nothing to hide behind. So, I press myself against the wall next to the door again. I wish I could press myself into that wall.

Then, I hear a noise, a voice I recognize.

Drago's.

What's he doing out there? Who's he talking to? He won't see me if he opens the door, but he will if he comes in and goes to the desk. I close my mouth and chomp down on my lips so I won't cry out by accident. I can still hear his voice but not what he's saying. I inch my way forward to stand right at the door again and put my ear to it.

"You're drunk. Return to your quarters." Ah, he's yelling at one of the crew. I slump with relief.

Whoever the drunk is mumbles something. It seems to make Drago angrier. There's another bam, and I hear him again.

"Come with me. You'll be facing the captain tomorrow. Whether you snuck the stuff on board or stole it from the passenger's lounge, I don't envy you."

I don't hear the rest, but it sounded like Drago had been shoving the sailor against the purser's door and is now pushing him down the companionway. If the drunk hadn't scared me so much, I'd feel sorry for him, having to face my father tomorrow. As it is, I hope he gets confined to quarters or has his pay docked or whatever my father does to punish being drunk.

I return to the desk, switch on the lamp again, open the copybook I brought with me and start writing. I'm halfway through the list when the lamp suddenly goes out. What happened? I swivel the chair around. *The door is still closed. Relax, Frankie,* I tell myself. *There's no one here besides you. The light bulb must have burned out, that's all.*

But there is still more to copy, and it's too dark to see anything, so dark I'm afraid that if I move, I'll bump into something. I know that on the wall to the right of the door is a light switch. I have to inch my way towards the wall, which I do without stumbling on anything. It's just like when I was lost in the warehouse in Baltimore, like playing Blind Man's Bluff. I run my hand over the wall until I feel the switch and turn it on. The light is so bright, I squeeze my eyes shut for a moment. So bright that someone might be able to see it in the companionway. What if Drago comes back?

No, I will not stop now. I return to the purser's desk and start writing the rest of the names.

I make it back to my cabin without running into anyone—no drunk sailors, no ghosts, no killers. There was only one problem. Since I returned the keys to my father's desk, I couldn't lock the door to the purser's office. But there was no way I was going to go back to my father's office, take the keys again, come back to lock the purser's door, and then return the keys to my father's desk. I've been lucky so far, but how long can that last? Suppose another drunk sailor comes stumbling down the companionway? The purser's door will have to stay closed but unlocked. I just have to hope he doesn't notice when he opens it in the morning.

CHAPTER 45

Frankie

The only line I didn't copy from the purser's log was the last column, "Next of Kin," which is the person my father has to call if a seaman gets hurt or dies. That means that he should have called the Wiper's nearest relative, but he couldn't because there was no next of kin written alongside the Wiper's name.

There are forty names on the list. The Wiper's is crossed out. Papa has put another date next to the date when he came on board—the day the police in Baltimore found his body.

He was Kristian Sisask, and he was from Estonia. It hits me that I never knew his name. To me, he was always just the Wiper. And I didn't know where he came from, either. I didn't feel it before, but now the fact that he was killed so far away from home makes me sad. He must have had a family back there, in Estonia. A mother and father, maybe? A little girl? Do they know that he's dead? Do they know he was murdered? Why didn't he give my father a name to put under the "Next of Kin" column?

I'll think about that later. I'll ask Danilo later, too, if the Wiper's family knows what happened to him. But I have to be careful. I'm not supposed to know his name was Kristian. With Danilo, I'll need to always say "the Wiper."

After I cross out my father's, Danilo's, and the Wiper's names, there are thirty-seven crew members left. The officers are listed separately, and the unlicensed seamen's names are listed under the department they work in, which is how I copied them.

OFFICERS

Name	Country	Date signed on	Position
Borowski, Feliks	Poland	12 October 1959	Engineer
Chiotis, Atalo	Greece	12 October 1959	Bosun
D'Antoni, Marco	Italy	12 October 1959	Elec. Officer
Doukakis, Stephanos	Greece	16 April 1958	Asst. Engineer
Dupnik, Anton	Czechoslovakia	16 April 1958	Electrician
Garafolo, Rocco	Italy	18 March 1956	Chief Mate
Giordini, Massimo	Italy	18 March 1956	Purser
Harma, Kaarel	Estonia	18 March 1956	Asst. Engineer
Levebre, Rene	France	18 March 1956	Radio Officer
~~Moretti, Flavio~~	~~Italy~~	~~18 March 1956~~	~~Captain~~
Nunziamo, Antonio	Italy	12 October 1959	Second Mate
Petrovic, Drago	Yugoslavia	12 October 1959	Third Mate
Vincenze, Rudolfo	Italy	6 April 1958	Engineer

UNLICENSED SEAMEN

Deck

Alessi, Georgio	Italy	12 October 1959
Benetiz, Osvaldo	Chile	29 January 1960
Campbell, Denzil	Jamaica	5 May 1959
Chastain, Albert	France	12 October 1959
Jensen, Magnus	Denmark	29 January 1960
Ndao, Robert	Senegal	16 April 1958
Nitschman, Edvard	West Germany	29 January 1960

Ricci, Giovanni	Italy	6 April 1958
Zello, Lorenzo	Italy	6 April 1958

Engine Room

Abato, Nicolo	Italy	12 October 1959
Catalini, Angelo	Italy	6 April 1958
Castillo, Andres	Venezuela	14 Febuary 1960
Dabo, Malik	Senegal	16 April 1958
Diouf, Louis	France	12 October 1959
Dupnik, Anton	Czechoslovakia	16 April 1958
Favale, Sergio	Italy	12 October 1959
~~Sisask, Kristian~~	~~Estonia~~	~~29 January 1960~~
~~(Deceased Febuary 12, 1960?)~~		

Mess

Bautista, Angelo	The Philippines	5 May 1959
Chourki, Hassan	Morocco	12 October 1959
Guinto, Modesto	The Philippines	5 May 1959
Lumamban, Arvin	The Philippines	29 January 1960
Mendozo, Efren	The Philippines	29 January 1960
Messina, Nello	Italy	12 October 1959
Ocampo, Rodel	The Philippines	18 March 1956
Peters, Winston	Jamaica	5 May 1959
Reid Joseph	Jamaica	5 May 1959
~~Ramos, Danilo~~	~~The Philippines~~	~~18 March 1956~~
Santos, Melchor	The Philippines	20 January 1960

First, I cross off the men not on shore leave on the day I was chased in New Orleans. Then, I go back and forth from country to date to country to date to country until I feel like I'm going cross-eyed. Maybe if I just put my head down on the desk for a couple of minutes …

My obnoxious cousin Ronald keeps on hitting the dogwood tree in the front yard with his baseball bat. "Don't," I yell at him. "You'll kill him. What's he ever done to you?"

"He cut open my mattress. Now I can't sleep. He deserves to die."

"The Dogwood tree didn't do it, Ronald. Don't you remember? Aunt Bess's knitting needles did. She used the blue one and the orange one and the mattress fell apart."

But Ronald doesn't stop. He keeps batting at that poor tree until my head falls off my body. When I try to pick it up, there's a paper stuck to my cheek. I pull it off, and my head snaps up.

I open my eyes wider and see the columns and my desk under them. Above it, the porthole. I feel my face and the top of my skull and my neck. They're all connected. And Ronald and the poor dogwood tree have disappeared. But I still hear the batting sound.

"Frankie, open the door." It's Danilo. I jump up and try to pull the door open. It's locked. Did I do that last night? I unlock and open it.

"Are you all right? Your father sent me. You're late for breakfast."

"I overslept, I guess. What time is it?"

"Almost 7:00. The captain had to go back to the bridge. He said he'll see you later, maybe at lunch."

Danilo looks at my face as though I have ketchup on my chin and then at the rest of me. I look, too. My skirt is turned so the zipper is in front, and my blouse is half in and half out of it.

"I was studying late last night. I must have fallen asleep at my desk." He's looking over at it now, but it's too far for him to see what I've written. He nods and turns to go.

"Well, you've got five minutes to get to the mess if you don't want to miss breakfast."

I don't, so I comb my hair, straighten my skirt, tuck in my blouse, and head to the mess. I'll brush my teeth later.

I gobble down my breakfast—scrambled eggs, toast, and today, a sausage patty instead of bacon. I'm the only one left in the officer's mess, which means that Winston has to wait for me to finish so he can clear the table. Usually, I like to talk to him, but not today. Today, I'm in a hurry. I have to get back to my cabin and to the list. There was something wrong last night when I looked at it, but I was too tired to figure out what it was.

Back at my desk, I see what's wrong. It looks like my bright idea wasn't so bright, more like one of the companionways when an overhead light is burned out.

I thought that if I could match up the country that the Wiper—no, Kristian—came from … if I could match it to the country of any of the other sailors, I could narrow the number of possible killers to three or four at the most. Then, all I had to do was look at the dates those three or four started serving on *Il Destino*, and whichever of them came from the same country and started on the same date as Kristian did would probably be the killer. Easy as pie.

It turns out only one of them is from Kristian's country, Kaarel Harma. He's been on *Il Destino* since it first sailed in 1956 when my father became its captain. Of course, that doesn't mean he couldn't be the killer. But if I add the date he started on *Il Destino* to the fact that he was on duty the day I was chased through New Orleans, I have to cross his name off. Other than him, no one, not a single crew member, is from Kristian's country.

I'm stumped! What a waste of time! I wonder what Miss Marple would do.

CHAPTER 46

The Dodger

A five-minute lecture on the responsibilities of a deckhand and how such an important job cannot be done by an inebriated seaman. The Dodger can't tell the captain that he's never been inebriated in his life, so he listens, a tinge of shame on his face and a slight hanging of his head, and watches as the captain writes his name in the logbook. The contrite sailor.

Then a warning. One more infraction and he'd be banished not only from *Il Destino* but from all the ships of the Vittoria Lines. This is the only point where the Dodger almost loses his contrite sailor mask and smiles. To his mind, that would be a reward, not a penalty.

Finally, the punishment for his offense of the night before. No shore leave when the ship reaches Naples. But he swears to himself that he will be going on shore in Naples, no matter what the captain says.

On shore and on his way home.

The Dodger is off duty, the lounge is empty and will be until the passengers arrive for their pre-dinner drinks. The last time, before he was finished searching here, he heard one of the crew coming and had to duck out the door that opens onto the deck. Now, he has an opportunity to complete that search. He has to take advantage of this opportunity for one last search to make sure he hadn't missed anything the last time. He is standing in front of the bar, running his hand along the hidden shelf below the counter when the captain's daughter walks in. Of course. Nowhere on the ship seems to be off limits to the girl.

The Dodger is about to lie to her about why he's there when she tells him she needs his help. Another opportunity to get her to trust him. He will need that trust if he has to kidnap her.

CHAPTER 47

Frankie

No one is helping me find the man who murdered Kristian. Certainly not Danilo. Every time I talk to him about it, I have to listen to his lecture about how dangerous it is looking for a murderer. I know being a chief steward is a job with a lot of responsibilities, but, really, you'd think he could at least try to help me. After all, I'm one of his responsibilities, too.

I can't talk to Papa, obviously. So, who does that leave? Not any of the officers. They'd report me to my father right away, even Drago.

That leaves the unlicensed seamen. Magnus, Edvard, Winston, and Osvaldo would all help me, I'm sure. But I must be very careful when I talk to each of them. It can't be where an officer might see me or when we might be interrupted. I also have to be careful not to let the seaman know why I'm asking my questions. After all, any one of them besides Winston could have killed Kristian.

And as I walk into the lounge, there's one right in front of me, standing at the bar with his back to me. Even better, he's one of my favorites. Actually, he's the handsomest sailor of all of them.

"Hello."

He jumps around. He looks startled to see me. I'd be startled to see him, too, if I weren't used to seeing him all over *Il Destino*. Then he smiles. What a smile. I wish he was younger; I'd smile back at him the same way.

"Good evening, Miss Francesca."

Should I ask him to look at the list? After all, there's nothing to say he couldn't be Kristian's killer. He was on shore leave the day I was chased through New Orleans. He's tall like the man I saw cutting open the mattress. But he's not from Estonia. On the other hand, the only other seaman from Estonia couldn't have been chasing me that day, so the killer has to be from a different country.

Still, this is my one chance of getting information from a crew member, so I'd better take it. I pull the list from the pocket of my skirt.

"I wonder if you would look at this for me."

"Of course, Miss. What is it?"

"A list of the crew on *Il Destino*."

"Are you looking for someone?" He raises his eyebrows and widens his eyes. They're a really light blue, lighter than the sky.

"No. I mean, *yes*. But I don't know who it is."

He laughs like he thinks it's funny. If he knew why I want him to look at it, he wouldn't laugh. He'd understand how important this is. But, just in case, I make something up, something that's serious but not the truth. I lie. Again.

"You know the Wiper?"

"The Italian?"

"No. Not him. The other one. The one who was killed in Baltimore."

He hunches up his shoulders and backs away from me like I'm going to spit on him. Could it be that he's afraid the same thing will happen to him? That surprises me. He's a big guy. I bet he could fight off anyone who tried to hurt him. Then he steps closer to me again.

"Why do you want to know about him?"

"Well, there wasn't any next of kin listed for him. So, I thought it would be a good idea to ask my father to have a little service for him and invite the Wiper's friends from the ship. Did you know him pretty well?"

"No. I hardly ever saw him. He worked in the engine room. I'm a deckhand." I know this. That's why it's a surprise to find him in the lounge. Maybe he's using it as a shortcut.

"So, what's the favor?"

"Would you look at this list and tell me if the Wiper was friends with any of the guys on it."

"Friends?"

"Yeah, you know, like eating with them or playing cards."

His smile is back. He puts out his hand. "Let me look at it."

I hand it to him, and he walks over to stand under a lamp on a side table. He holds the list in one hand and runs the middle finger of the other down the names written there. I guess where he's from that's not impolite. He looks up at me and smiles again, then walks back to where I'm standing and holds the list out between us.

"He worked with this one." He points to Malik Dabo. "They were always on duty together. And this one." He points to Lorenzo Zello. "I saw them in the mess together. A lot."

His middle finger keeps moving down the paper.

"Oh, and this one here, the Jamaican. They seemed to be good friends. They played poker together a lot."

How does he know all this if he hardly ever saw Kristian?

"Anybody else?"

He takes another look at the list from the top to the bottom, points to one more, then starts to hand it back to me.

"Those are the only ones I remember." He pulls the hand holding the list back to his chest. "I have an idea." He folds the list up and puts it in his pocket. "Let me take this and ask around. He might have had other friends I don't know about."

I start to ask him to give the list back, then decide that it doesn't matter. I have another copy in my cabin. Anyway, I hear someone coming.

CHAPTER 48

The Dodger

She asks the Dodger if he knew Sisask, and although he doesn't expect the question, he doesn't change his expression. She hands him a list, says she wants to organize a service for a dead sailor just because he doesn't have a next of kin listed beside his name.

Doesn't she have anything better to do? He'd like to ask her, but he knows the answer. No, she doesn't. Typical, in his opinion. In his country, she would be farming or working in a factory, doing something useful to society. She wouldn't be allowed to waste time on such frivolities. And does she really think the captain and the other officers will go along with holding this service? Is she that stupid? Maybe, but he can sense that something's not right. If she really wanted to do what she says, she could ask her babysitter, the chief steward, for this information. What's she really up to?

He points to a few names, makes up some story about seeing each of them with Sisask, and starts to give the list back to her. Then, he changes his mind and puts it in his pocket, saying he'll study it and ask some of the other men if they know who he was friends with. He's about to suggest she meet him later tonight when he hears someone coming.

"We just have time for a quick cocktail before dinner," the Dodger hears one of the male passengers say. The girl runs to the door of the lounge and intercepts whoever it is before he enters the lounge.

"Hello, Mr. Manucci."

"Well, hello, young lady. Are you serving drinks tonight?" The man laughs at his own joke. The girl laughs, too.

"No, Sir. But I'll get the steward for you." Before the passenger can enter the lounge, the Dodger slips out through the door opposite.

CHAPTER 49

Frankie

I'm sitting on my bunk, staring at my newest list of suspects, Kristian's four friends. What am I supposed to do with them? I fling myself back on the mattress. I want to give up.

Then I remember something Mom used to say when I felt this way, like when I'd toss my recorder on the sofa because I couldn't get the notes right. "Don't be a quitter," she would say. "Be like your Papa. There were a lot of times when he could have given up, but he never did. If he had, you wouldn't be here."

I jump up from my bunk and carry a copy of the list to my desk and check the four names against it. If I can take Aunt Bess's advice, then I sure can take my own mother's. I will be like my Papa; I won't quit. I only have to figure out where to go from here.

So, I sit, staring at the four names, then cross off all but one. It couldn't be Malik Dabo or Lorenzo Zello. Neither of them could have chased me through New Orleans because they weren't on shore leave. They were both on *Il Destino* that day. A breakthrough in my investigation. Hurrah! Albert Chastain, a deck hand, is pretty old. He must be at least forty. Probably too old to run as fast as whoever was chasing me. And he's not tall. That only leaves the fourth seaman on the list, Denzil Campbell. He's tall, but not as tall as I remember the guy who was cutting the mattress. I'll keep him on the list, though. Maybe I'm remembering wrong.

It looks like another waste of time. It's so frustrating. No one seems to fit.

I'm hungry. Maybe once I have something in my stomach, I can figure it out.

CHAPTER 50

Frankie

Dinner with the passengers was fun tonight. Mr. Manucci told us the story of his first day on his first job out of high school. He was working for a company that renovated houses, and training to be a plumber. His boss had asked him to attach a new faucet in a bathroom. When Mr. Manucci took off the old faucet, he forgot to turn off the main water supply valve. His hands flew all through the air as he described water spurting up like a volcano erupting and trying to plug it up with a towel that got soaked and his boss walking in and seeing him and firing him. It wouldn't have been so funny except Mr. Manucci had so much fun telling it and his boss ended up hiring him back. And eventually, Mr. Manucci made a lot of money with his own plumbing supply business, the largest in Houston, he says.

Everybody laughed, even my father. Well, not everybody. Mr. Jerome just smiled. But that was a lot for him. They all seemed to have forgotten the storm and their seasickness.

When I get back to my cabin, the list I made is waiting for me. I keep staring at it, but it doesn't help me come up with any ideas. I feel like if I read it again, I'll get cross-eyed.

My idea for a motive—that Kristian and the man who murdered him knew each other before coming on board—may be a dud. Copying the crew list hasn't worked. It's like when Tricia and I saved our allowance for three months and then took the bus all the way downtown to see The Divots sing at that nightclub, and the guy at the door said we were too young and to come back in ten years. He was nice about it, but the guy who caught us trying to slip in through the alley door wasn't.

I'm going to bed. I'm not going to read myself to sleep with Agatha Christie either. Not tonight.

Was it a fog horn that woke me up? Or a giant wave hitting the ship? Or was it a dream?

I sit up. It was a dream. My cousin Ronald was lying to Aunt Bess about something. What was it? I know! She accused him of going to Kenny Perkins' house. Aunt Bess doesn't approve of Kenny Perkins because his parents are divorced. She thinks there's not enough "supervision" there, so Ronald lied to her.

"I was at the library," he said, "studying all the countries in the world for my geography test."

All the countries in the world. There are so many. It would be easy for a sailor to say he's from one of them when he really isn't. I mean, if a person could murder another human being, he could just as easily lie about where he's from. Of course, he would only do that if he knew before he signed on that he was going to be murdering one of his countrymen.

Maybe my idea would work, after all.

But I still have to find out who lied. I plop back down on my pillow and rest the back of my head on the palms of my hands. Moonlight is pouring in through the porthole. I gaze up at the ceiling. Maybe if I concentrate hard enough, the answer will appear there.

Five bells wakes me like it does every morning at 6:30. I can hear the deck hands laughing and calling to each other. Sometimes in English, sometimes in Italian, sometimes in their native languages.

I've got it! Languages! I throw myself onto my stomach and hug the pillow. That's the way I can find out if each sailor really is from where he says. I can test the crew. I can ask each of them what language he speaks in his own country. Then, I can ask him to say something to me in that language.

I punch the pillow. That's stupid. There's no way that would work. First, I'm only allowed to talk to the officers, and the man who killed Kristian might not be an officer. Still, if I sneak around, which I'm getting pretty good at, I could probably manage to talk to most of the crew, especially the taller ones, without my father finding out.

There's another problem, though. The only languages I know are English and Italian and a little bit of Spanish from school. How could I tell the difference between German and Greek? Or between Estonian and whatever they speak in Senegal?

I give the pillow another poke. I need to find a different way.

But first, I need to get some breakfast.

After breakfast, I start to plan. The first thing I have to find out is if any of the seamen on shore leave in New Orleans that day are really from Estonia, like Kristian. Or are they lying about it. And I can even shorten that list if I concentrate on the ones who are tall.

There's Denzil. The logbook says he's from Jamaica. He's sort of tall, and he looks a lot more like Winston than he does like Harvel Kaarma. Is that enough information to eliminate him? Maybe. Maybe not. Winston could probably tell. But I can't tell him why I need to know. I guess I could ask him, casual-like, "Hello, Winston. I was wondering—did you know Denzil when you lived in Jamaica?" He might say, "Sure. We grew up in the same neighborhood." Or, "Are you kidding, Miss? Do you know how many people live in Jamaica?"

But suppose he says, "Jamaica? Denzil isn't from Jamaica. Can't you tell by his accent?" And if I'm really lucky, he might say, "Can't you tell by his accent that he's from Estonia?"

The more I think about it, the more I realize that there are only two reasons Denzil is on my suspect list. One is that he was on shore leave that day in New Orleans. The other is that he was a friend of Kristian's. But was he really? It's not saying much that they played cards with each other. There are probably other sailors that Kristian played cards with, and a lot of sailors that he worked with. After all, only one crew member said they were friends, and he's a deckhand and said himself that he didn't know Kristian well. And, if I'm honest, he would be more likely to be the killer than Denzil. Because there were five tall crew members on leave that day, two officers—the first mate and Drago—and three unlicensed seamen—Oswaldo, Edvard, and Magnus. I'd like it to be the first mate because I don't like him and he obviously hates me, but he probably didn't hate Kristian. Did any of the others?

It could be Drago, I suppose. Just because he's an officer doesn't mean he can't be a murderer, too. But Drago doesn't look very Estonian, either. He has dark hair, tanned skin, and brown eyes, like my father's. But I'd better not cross him off the list just because of that.

Then there's Osvaldo and Edvard and Magnus. All three were on shore leave that day, and all of them were late getting back to *Il Destino*.

Oh, all this thinking is making my brain tired. I'll do my homework. That's gotta be easier.

CHAPTER 51

Frankie

Il Destino is surrounded by fog. I've never seen anything like it. It's so gray and thick that when I look through the porthole, it looks like a mass of dirty cotton balls. I definitely won't be walking on deck in this stuff. My homework is done, and my father will be on the bridge as long as it stays this foggy. The passengers are dressing for dinner, and Danilo and the cooks and stewards are busy preparing to serve dinner. On this whole ship, there's no one for me to talk to.

I wish I could call Tricia or Ellen, even Peter. No, not Peter. I've been gone a long time, long enough for him to find a new girlfriend. Definitely Tricia. I have so much to tell her. I started to write her when we docked in New Orleans, so I could mail the letter there, but then my father told me I'd be going back to Baltimore, where I'd see her anyway. I'll have to send her a letter from Naples. I know she's never gotten a letter from there before.

Might as well take a walk below deck. Maybe it will help clear my head and solve the case of the Wiper's murder.

Il Destino must be traveling at about half its normal speed, and the only sound seems to be the fog horn. Otherwise, it's much quieter down here than usual. I can actually hear the clomp of my saddle shoes. If only I had a pair of tennis shoes, I wouldn't make a sound as I walk along the companionways.

I pass the bosun's store and look in. No one's there. Then the steward's store. No one's there, either. I see nobody as I walk along the Number 5 and Number 4 'tween decks.

Think like Miss Marple or Monsieur Poirot, Frankie. What have I failed to ask myself about this investigation?

One: Since none of the suspects are from Kristian's country, does it mean that my theory is wrong that they knew each other before? Not necessarily. It could mean that the killer lied about his nationality, or that he knew Kristian from somewhere else, from serving on another ship together, maybe. If the killer really did lie about where he was from, it could be because he thought my father would never hire a seaman from the killer's real country. Or maybe he didn't want Kristian to know they were the same nationality for some reason.

For that matter—I stop in the middle of the stairs—Kristian could have lied, too. Of course, he could.

What is question number two? Opportunity. How did the killer find the opportunity to murder Kristian and to chase me through New Orleans? I know the answer to the second part of that question. He was on shore leave; he could have followed me all day if he wanted to. So, since Kristian's body was found behind a tavern near the wharf instead of on *Il Destino*, the killer must have been on shore leave at the same time. That was the day before I came aboard. Where can I find out who was on leave that day? In the ship's log? I think I'm going to have to ask Danilo and hope he keeps his promise not to tell my father what I'm doing.

I pause outside the door of the galley, which is the best-smelling place on the ship, especially when Nello Messina is cooking, like tonight.

Stop thinking about food and concentrate on the murder, Frankie. What is question number three? Motive. Why did the actress in *The Mirror Cracked* poison that lady? Why did that woman in *Peril at End House* kill her cousin? The first one was out of revenge. The second one was for money. I guess the killer could have been avenging something Kristian did in the past. He could also have wanted Kristian's money, or money that Kristian owed him but wouldn't pay back. The only way to find out what I wonder about is to ask the killer—and I'd have to catch him to do that.

Are there any other questions? Probably, but I can't think of them now. Maybe after dinner. I always think better on a full stomach.

Danilo is having a hard time. The passengers are especially demanding tonight. Maybe it's the fog. For one thing, the Churches and the Manuccis are disappointed that my father and the other officers didn't join them for dinner.

Then, Mr. Church sends his steak back because, he says it's overcooked even though it looks almost raw to me. Mr. Manucci keeps asking why we don't serve more Italian food, considering that *Il Destino* is an Italian ship. When Danilo explains that two of the choices at each dinner are Italian, Mr. Manucci looks at the menu card and says, "Show me a single Italian dish on this menu." After Danilo points out the Seafood Risotto and the Osso Buco and explains that both dishes are served in Italy, Mrs. Manucci tells her husband that there is more to Italian cooking than spaghetti and meatballs. He mumbles something about lasagna and orders a steak.

By the time Mr. Church's second steak and Mr. Manucci's first one arrive, it's past three bells. By the time the passengers finish their desserts and have their after-dinner drinks, it's forty-five minutes later than usual. I'll never get a chance to ask Danilo tonight about who was on shore leave in Baltimore.

For once, I'm glad to get out of the saloon.

I spent the afternoon concentrating on my mystery, and I don't like what I've concluded—that it has to be one of five men—Edvard, Osvaldo, Magnus, Drago, or Officer Garafolo. I want Officer Garafolo to be the guilty one.

I turn left out of the saloon and pass the lounge. With this fog, I could walk right off the deck and into the ocean if I'm not careful, so I open a hatch and go below deck, thinking the whole time. *Okay, down to five suspects.*

Drago? Yes, he was on shore leave that day in New Orleans. But when he returned to the ship, he was with two other officers. Was he with them all day? If so, he couldn't have been chasing me. Still, I can't rule him out until I know for certain. He might have run into the other two at the gate to the port and walked back to the ship with them. Drago stays on my list.

Osvaldo? He returned to *Il Destino* late that day, and he was alone. Plus, he says he's from Chile, but is he really? I think South Americans have dark hair. Osvaldo's hair is red. So, he could be from Estonia. But wouldn't the other seamen who speak Spanish catch on if that were the case? Of course, they would, so if he's the killer, it wouldn't be because he knew Kristian in Estonia.

I walk along the companionway past the fridge lockers. The fog is so thick is creeps inside the ship, and I pass through puffs of it as I move along.

Then there's Edvard. Like Osvaldo, he returned to *Il Destino* alone and late. But all those Snickers bars he gives me? They don't mean anything. He could have given them to me just to stay on the good side of the captain's daughter. And he's the only one on the ship from West Germany, which means there aren't any other Germans to notice if his accent is peculiar.

Magnus? Like Osvaldo and the rest, he's tall. Like Edvard, language wouldn't be a problem for him. He's the only seaman on *Il Destino* from Denmark, or so he says, so he wouldn't have to worry about another seaman from there catching him lying about his nationality.

Finally, there's the first mate. The problem is he's not from Estonia, and he's also served on *Il Destino* since it first sailed. What would his motive be for killing Kristian?

I climb down the ladder to the No. 2 'tween deck.

How about their actions on board? Are any of them acting strangely? Since I didn't know any of them except the first mate before we left Baltimore, I can't answer that question.

But I have seen one of them doing something out of the ordinary, and more than once. Since the day we left the port of Baltimore, I've run into him almost everywhere on *Il Destino*. Not just on deck where he works, or in the mess where he eats, but standing around the life-boats not doing anything, outside the radio room and the engine room crew's quarters. And in the saloon. Could that explain the funny way he acted when I showed him the crew list? It could. And he did keep that list instead of giving it back to me. If we hadn't been interrupted by Mr. Manucci and I had asked for it back, would he have given it to me? I'm not sure he would have.

I sit down suddenly on a step. It's Edvard. I know it. But why? I can't go by my instincts; I have to use reason—just like my two favorite amateur detectives—and look at the evidence.

First: The crew list says Edvard is from West Germany, and since he's the only crew member from there, no one could catch him if he didn't speak German or if he spoke it with the wrong accent. Second: If I go by his looks alone, he could easily be from a country in northern Europe. Third: He was in New Orleans on the right day and got back to the ship late. Fourth—I hadn't thought of this before—he joined the crew at the same time as Kristian. Fifth: He acted funny when I asked him to look at the list. Sixth: He said he hardly ever saw Kristian, then gave me the names of four seamen he says he saw Kristian with a lot. And the last one—he's always wandering around *Il Destino* and being in places he has no right to be.

Yes, it's Edvard, all right. My reason tells me so and so does my gut.

Another question: Should I tell my father about this? He'd want proof, and I don't really have any. What would I say: "Well, Papa, I've come to the conclusion that Edvard murdered Kristian?" I can just imagine what he'd say, and it wouldn't be, "All right, Francesca, I'll have him arrested right away."

I should return to my cabin to figure out what to do next, but I think better when I'm walking. Maybe I'll go down to the engine room. It's far away from where Edvard works, and there's always crew there.

CHAPTER 52

The Dodger

H is plan worked. The engine room is empty.

The Dodger was beginning to worry that he'd timed it wrong. It was supposed to be fast-acting, but it took almost six hours. But when, from his hiding place across from the engine room, he saw the chief engineer run up the ladder out of the engine room, followed by the electrician and the new Wiper, he knew he would be alone for what he hoped would be a long time. It wasn't easy, but he made sure there was plenty of the stuff in the coffee they drank before they came on duty.

Now that he has the engine room to himself, he wonders where to start. There are hundreds of pieces of machinery here—the engine itself, generators, pumps, pipelines everywhere, a propeller shaft, a control console, tanks, hatches along the wall, all of them on two levels. What the rest of the machines are, he can't guess. He would need a whole day to search this place. At best, he only has two hours.

With the engine room noise, he knows he'd never hear someone returning. He feels like he's standing at the ocean's edge in a hurricane, the wind and waves combining to shut out every other sound on earth. And it's hot and shadowy and claustrophobic. Another reason he must hurry.

He looks at the machines eight feet over his head. He'll need to climb a ladder to search up there and decides to save that until last—if he has enough time.

He searches for almost an hour, checking behind every dial, and behind, above, and below every machine he can. His eyes are burning, and his handkerchief is now too wet to control the sweat dripping down his forehead. If that traitor Sisask were in front of him now, the Dodger swears he'd kill him all over again for putting him in this place.

He keeps searching, stopping every few minutes to make sure a crew member isn't climbing down the ladder. When he squeezes his body behind another of the mystery machines, he sees something interesting: a trap door in the floor next to a wall. He leans down and pulls it open. It's not as heavy as he thought it would be. Quickly, he lowers himself inside and looks around. The room is small, even for a ship, around 5'x 6'. He has to stoop to prevent hitting his head on the ceiling.

At first, he sees nothing, no place where the document could be hidden. Then he peers closely at the floor and spots it. Another trap door, this one opening to a space much smaller—just large enough for a human hand, not large enough for a human body.

He kneels and tries to open it. He tugs, but it doesn't budge. He tugs harder and is thrown back when the door bursts open. He gets on his knees and crawls to the opening. He thrusts his hand into the hole and probes to the right and left, then forward and backward until it brushes against something that feels like oil cloth. He pulls it out. It looks like the drawstring purses carried by the prostitutes in their last port. When he unties it and looks inside, he sees what he's been searching for ever since coming aboard.

The document.

The Dodger would like to read it to find out why it's so vital that it be found. But someone might return any second. So, he climbs out through the trap door. As he weaves through the boilers, tanks, pumps and generators, he sticks the document between his chest and sweater. It may get a little wet with his sweat but not too damaged. The boss told the Dodger he wants to see it, and if the boss doesn't see it for himself, he won't believe the Dodger really found it.

The next step is to keep it safe until the ship reaches Naples. He needs a place where there's no chance of it being found by one of the others but where he can easily retrieve it when the ship reaches port. He can't put it back in the hole beneath the trap door of the engine room. That only succeeded as a hiding place for the Wiper because he worked there every day. It won't work for the Dodger because he won't have another opportunity to be there alone. He's run out of laxatives.

But he has the document. That's all that matters.

CHAPTER 53

Frankie

I move down the stairs, but not too fast. I walk down the companion-way, then down another flight. The noise gets louder the closer I get. Even in the quiet of the fog, it drowns out the clumping sound of my shoes. When I come to the top of the ladder to the engine room and look down, I don't see anyone there.

I call, but no one answers. This is strange. Actually, it's worse than strange. Both my father and the chief engineer told me that the engine room is manned at all times. I hate to be a snitch, but I should let one of the officers know.

I'm about to leave when I do see someone. He appears suddenly from around the back of that big metal machine that has all the wheels sticking out of it. It's too dark to tell who he is. There are a lot of shadows in the engine room, so many that all I can tell is that he's sticking something under his sweater. Should I take a chance that it's one of the officers and say, "Hi"?

I'd best not. Something tells me that I'd better get back to my cabin right away.

CHAPTER 54

The Dodger

The Dodger scuttles up the ladder to the companionway and stops. He glimpses a movement to his right and turns toward it, his heart thumping at the thought that one of the engine room crew has returned. His mind is swirling with choices. Does he think up another excuse for being there? Does he knock out whoever it is and hope that person won't remember what he saw when he comes to? Or does he kill him and make it look like an accident?

Before the Dodger has decided, his mind registers who it is. The captain's daughter. Her back is to him, and she's starting up the stairs from the companionway to the 'tween deck. What's she doing here? More important: Has she seen him?

She looks around.

She's seen him now.

The look she gives the Dodger is so different from the way she used to look at him. She looks frightened. Why?

Anyway, why should he worry? She can't have any idea what he's up to. The only trouble is, her father is the captain. If she says something to him, the captain might get suspicious. But even if she tells her father she thinks something's wrong with the Dodger, the captain probably wouldn't pay any attention, not to an overly imaginative teenager like her.

But why, now, is she suddenly shying away from him instead of following him as she did before? He can think of nothing he said or did that would make her act that way. He slowly moves toward her.

Then her look changes, sharpens, focuses on the Dodger. The fear is still there and something else, something he can't work out. She turns and starts to climb up to the 'tween deck.

He has to stop her.

CHAPTER 55

Frankie

The pain is horrible. It's even worse than when I was thirteen and the horse that was supposed to be so gentle decided to gallop away from the others and throw me forward over his head. Nothing was broken, but everything hurt then and everything hurts now.

Only now, it's worse because I can't see anything. This is the darkest place I've ever been. There's nothing wrong with my ears, though. I can hear loud banging. But I can't tell where it's coming from.

When I turn my head, I figure out why it's so dark. I'm blindfolded. Not only that. My hands and feet are tied. I feel like I'm going to throw up, but there's something jammed in my mouth, so I try very hard not to. How did I end up like this? I still don't know where I am or what's making the noise or why my body hurts so much.

Then I remember. The man who came out of the engine room. It was Edvard. He saw me, and I tried to get away, but he caught up with me. I don't know what happened next. Did he knock me out and when I was unconscious, tie me up and put me—where?

Well, at least, now I know that I was right to suspect him. He's the one who killed Kristian. Edvard, so handsome with his sky-blue eyes and Troy Donahue hair. Edvard, who was always sneaking me Snickers bars when I walked on deck. I swear, I will never eat another Snickers in my life.

And who did I ask for help when I wanted to know who Kristian's friends were? Edvard. He must have guessed that I wasn't really asking to arrange a service for Kristian. He must have started to suspect I knew something. Somehow, he read my mind.

No, I probably gave it away when I ran away from him, like in New Orleans. But this time he was right behind me, so I didn't get far. If my hands weren't tied up, I'd hit myself in the head and make it hurt even more. News bulletin, Frankie: You're not as smart as you thought you were. I waited too long. I didn't tell my father; I didn't tell Danilo. Now, they might never find out that it was Edvard who killed Kristian, and they might never find me.

I'm sweating and my heart is beating too fast. I feel like I'm going to faint.

And Papa? He'll think I fell overboard in the fog. He'll blame himself when he should blame me. And the worst thing is that he will be alone. He already lost his wife, and now his daughter will be lost, too. How could I have done this to him?

Please, God, no! Please don't let me die in here. Please don't let my poor Papa be left all alone. Help me, God. I am crying so hard, the blindfold is soaked through and snot is dripping down to my lips. But I keep on praying.

Just take a deep breath and calm down, young lady. Aunt Bess? Yes, she said that to me more than once. Well, this time I will listen. I take deep breaths, one after another, until the crying stops and I can think. I need to calm down. Papa will search for me. He'll search for me until he finds me. I relax—a little.

I won't leave Papa all by himself, without a family. I will get out of here. I can handle this. I can beat Edvard. Simple. Easy peasy. No problem at all. You've just got to think, Frankie.

So, first, where am I?

Not in my cabin. My cabin doesn't smell like this, sort of like my cousin Ronald's room gets over the weekend when his dirty socks and underpants have been lying in the corner too long and the plate from his banana and peanut butter sandwich has been under his bed since Friday night. Wherever it's coming from, the smell makes me want to throw up again.

The noise. Now that I think about it, it's not so much a *bang, bang, bang,* as a *thump, thump, thump.* Like an engine. But I can't be in the engine room because my head is touching one wall and my feet are pushed up against another. Too small for the engine room. And not as loud either.

Then I get it. It's that space under the trap door the chief engineer showed me. It was small and gray and damp and cramped. Nothing is in it, he told me, and they never use it. That means there's no reason for anybody to check it. Ever.

Except Edvard. He'll come back and kill me, just like he killed Kristian.

CHAPTER 56

Edvard

Edvard is pleased with himself. The girl is taken care of, at least for the time being. But what happens when her father realizes she's missing? He will send every seaman he can spare to look for her. Will they think about the trap door in the engine room? If they do, she'll tell them that he put her there. She won't know why, but that doesn't matter. He will still be in custody, and the captain will turn him over to the Italian police when the ship reaches Naples.

Should he have killed her when he had the chance? Yes. Once he'd found the document, he no longer needed her alive to use as a hostage. But he was in a hurry to get out of the engine room before anyone returned and to put the document some place safe but easy to retrieve when the ship reached Naples. Leaving her alive was a mistake. He hopes he doesn't end up regretting it.

Anyway, there is still time. Time to kill her and throw her overboard if necessary. Then, when no one can find her, they'll think there was an accident, that she was on deck when she shouldn't have been, stumbled in the fog, and fell into the sea.

But he will have to find a way to get back into the engine room and get her out—without anyone seeing.

First, though, he has to hide the envelope. Once they realize she's missing, every seaman will be a suspect in her disappearance and may be searched. If they find the envelope on him, they will guess that he's the one responsible.

He makes his way toward the galley.

CHAPTER 57

Frankie

It's not so hard to scoot backwards, I'm finding out. My stupid saddle shoes don't seem so stupid any more. The bottoms are rubbery enough to make it easy to push myself up on the wall in back of me.

I will throw away this skirt, though. If my aunt had let me wear blue jeans, then the floor wouldn't feel so rough and cold under my bottom. But I've got to keep on scooting. I have to get out of here before Edvard returns. I yank against the rope around my wrists. It's too tight; I can't wriggle out of it. Same with my ankles. The blindfold is a problem, too. I try to use my shoulder to push it off my eyes but can't get my head that low.

So, I keep on scooting backwards and use my feet to push until I'm sitting up higher.

If I can get my shoes off, I might be able to slide my feet through the rope. But it's not easy with my ankles tied together. I put the heel of my right foot on top of the instep part of my left shoe and push down. After seven or eight times, the shoe falls off. Then I put my left heel on the instep part of my right shoe. That goes a little faster.

I'm afraid it's not fast enough, though. When is Edvard coming back?

Stop wasting time thinking about that, Frankie. Concentrate on getting out of this hole. If I can just push the rope over my ankles and down my feet, I'll be able to stand and walk out of here. Except—

Except that I can't see where I'd be walking.

It doesn't matter, anyway. The rope around my ankles is too tight to move. It shouldn't surprise me. Sailors know all about ropes, and Edvard is a sailor. Or is he?

My socks give me less traction than my shoes did, but I eventually squirm backwards some more and sit up even higher. Now my head is really pounding, and my heart feels like it's going to jump out of my chest. No time to think about that. When Edvard returns, I have to be ready for him. Or better, I have to not be here.

My fingers feel the wall. It's rough like the floor, but warm, almost hot. I turn my sweaty face and wet blindfold to it and rub it up the wall's surface. The blindfold moves down an inch, so I keep rubbing my head up to get it to move down some more. The wall scratches, and my forehead and cheek feel wet. Blood. I stop for a moment. It's just a couple of drops; it's not like I'm bleeding to death, I tell myself. And if I don't get out of here soon, there will be a lot more blood—and it will all be mine.

I start rubbing again.

Then the blindfold is off, hanging around my neck. It doesn't do much good. The room is almost as dark with the blindfold off as it was with it on. But there's enough light to see my wrists and the rope so tight around them. How can I ever get them unknotted?

The noise is even louder now and throbbing, sort of like my heart. I wonder if maybe that's where my headache is coming from.

Stop thinking about your headache, Frankie. Think about escaping. Think about Papa and how horrible it would be for him if you die. So, what do I do now?

First, I have to get out whatever it is that Edvard jammed into my mouth. I hate to think what might happen if I throw up with that thing in my mouth. I use my tongue to try to push it out. It moves a little, but it's still jammed in there. I lean down to my wrists. If I can only use my fingers to pull it out. I raise the middle finger of my right hand and put it in the side of my mouth to try to push it out that way. I start to gag, so I pull my finger out and take deep breaths through my nose. I try again with my left hand on the other side of my mouth, pulling my lips close to my cheek. I gag again, but this time I don't stop trying to push the cloth out. When I gagged, my tongue pushed it out a little. Yes, that's what I need to do—use my tongue. I keep using it to push and keep gagging while I'm doing it. I start to choke, then cough. The cough was good; it pushes the cloth out a little more.

I lean toward my hands again. The cloth is out far enough that I can grip it with my thumb and forefinger. The cloth is soaked, but this is good because I can grip it tightly. I pull, then pull again. It slides out and with it, some vomit, but I don't care about the vomit. Now I have a chance because I can yell for help.

I yell and yell, louder and louder. Nothing happens. No one comes. Is the engine room still empty, or is it that no one can hear me? I'm afraid it's that they can't hear me. I can yell all day and night, and no one is going to come and get me.

I've got to get the rope off my wrists. How? My teeth? I lean over and bite down on the rope. I try to chew it. It's really thick, but I keep trying. It's no use. A German Shepherd couldn't chew through it.

I'm stuck here. No one will ever know where I am and who put me here. I give up. I will starve to death in this awful hole. Oh, Papa. I'm sorry. I say this out loud, over and over, even through my sobs. Oh, Mom, what have I done?

You've given up, and that is not like you, Frankie.

"Mom, is that you? Mom?" There's no answer. Did I really hear her? Yes. And she's angry with me because I've given up. I stay still for a few seconds, and then I'm back to the Frankie she knows. "Yes, Mom. You're right. I won't give up." I take some more deep breaths and try to think.

So, my teeth didn't do the trick. What will? The wall? The rough wall that helped me get the blindfold off? I have to try.

I wriggle around so my left arm is against the wall and yank my hands so they are pressed against it. Then, I start to rub. Up and down and back and forth. I don't stop, not even when my left wrist starts to bleed. I rub and rub until my arms ache so much I can hardly lift them up and down. Then, I rub some more. I'm still crying. But I haven't given up. The blood, the pain—they don't matter. What matters is escaping and finding my father so he can arrest Edvard.

I takes me a few seconds to realize that it worked—the rope has frayed away, and my hands are free. I use my shaky left hand and my teeth—I don't know what my dentist would say—to get the rope completely off my right wrist.

Now, my feet.

CHAPTER 58

Frankie

I did it! I'm bleeding, but I did it. I thought he'd be back before I could, but now my hands and feet are free. I can walk out of here before Edvard returns.

I get up on my hands and knees, but the pain is not just in my head anymore. My arms are sore, and my legs are all cramped up. How long was I unconscious, anyway? I rub my arms, then the calves of my legs. They still hurt but it's a little better so I can concentrate on getting out of this hole.

All I have to do is push open the trap door above me and—

It's not budging. Okay, I've got a better idea. No blindfold and no ropes means I can bang on the trap door and yell for help. The engine room crew must be back by now; they will hear me and let me out.

I bang and bang and start screaming like some stupid girl in a horror movie who decides to enter the spooky house all alone and then is surprised that a monster is in there waiting for her. I stop and wait for the door to open. Nothing. Maybe the crew isn't back yet. Or maybe the noise in the engine room is so loud, they can't hear me. I bang again with my fists. I scream even louder than the stupid girl in the horror movie and keep on screaming until my screams turn to sobs.

I fall back against the wall and pull my knees up against my face. I can't stop crying. Why doesn't anyone wonder where I am? Doesn't anyone care?

Now, my Mom's voice is back. *Stop feeling sorry for yourself, Frankie. It's not the end of the world.* It might be, though. It might be the end of *my* world if I don't get out of here. But Mom's right. I *am* feeling sorry for myself, and I need to stop it and start thinking again. Now! After all, I am Frankie Moretti, the girl who doesn't quit.

Yes, people on this ship do care about me, and they are looking for me. If I wait long enough, someone's bound to find me here. If they remember this hole. But what if they don't? No, I can't wait for them to find me.

I push up on the trap door with my hand again. It still doesn't budge. Because it's locked? Because it's heavy? If it's locked, I can't do anything about it. But if it's only heavy? I will just have to push it harder—and with something stronger than my hands.

My legs! I rode my bike almost every day in Baltimore, so they're strong, right?

Okay, here I go.

CHAPTER 59

Edvard

E dvard has put the document in a safe place. Now, it's time to deal with the girl. He had planned to leave her there. He wasn't going to chance being caught in the engine room again. She wouldn't have any water or food. Maybe she would be dead by the time the ship reaches Naples tomorrow. Maybe not.

But he knows he can't wait that long. The captain or the Filipino is bound to miss her soon and set up a search. He has to get back into the engine room and do what he should have done right away—kill her. If he had, no one would have seen him toss her over the rail, not in that thick fog. Now *Il Destino* has sailed through it, and it will be impossible for him to carry her on deck and dispose of her with no one noticing.

So, how can he get rid of her?

Then the solution to his problem hits him. The means of disposing of her are right there, right above her in the engine room. Not drowning. No need to carry her body through the companionways, up the ladders and across the deck, taking the risk of running into someone. No need to hoist her over the railing and toss her in the water.

The answer is not water. The answer is fire. Easy to burn something in an engine room. There's an incinerator right there. He heads back to the engine room.

He will still need access, though, and without anyone seeing him. How? He will figure it out. He did it before; he can do it again.

CHAPTER 60

Frankie

When I stagger around the boiler, my legs are sore from the job they did in finally knocking open the trap door. The electrician makes the sign of the cross, and the greaser grabs at his chest. I guess they weren't expecting to see me there. And, until a few minutes ago, I wasn't expecting to see them, either. Or anyone else. Ever.

I don't stop to talk to them. It would be too hard to explain why I'm here. Anyway, from the looks on their faces—I'd never noticed that the electrician had so many gold fillings before—I doubt that they'd understand any explanation I could give them. So, I just smile, give a little curtsy, and run up the ladder.

I continue to run, down the companionway and up the next set of stairs. Edvard could be anywhere. Down here. On deck. I could meet him, and he could hit me again, and maybe this time, throw me overboard.

When I reach my father's cabin, I don't knock. I push open the door and rush in. Please let him be here, I pray. He's not.

Is he still on the bridge? To find out, I'll have to go on deck, and Edvard could be there.

I guess I could stay here, lock the door, and wait until Papa returns. But I don't know how long that will be. I don't know if I can stand sitting here alone—even with the door locked. Edvard's strong. He could probably knock it down in two seconds.

I have to chance rushing to the bridge to find my father. He'll protect me. Papa isn't afraid of anybody, especially a lying, killing snake like Edvard.

I open the door and peek out. No one's there. The puffs of fog are gone. I pull the door closed behind me, run down the companionway, jump over the coaming, and rush through the hatch that will take me to the ladder leading to the weather deck. When I reach it, I stop. My hand is on the handle—'the dog,' they call it. I only have to push it down and shove the hatch open. But Edvard could be on the other side, and if he sees me before I see him, if he grabs me and throws me back down the ladder or over the rail into the ocean? Could he do that without anyone noticing?

I grab the dog so tightly that my wrist starts to bleed again. I try to calm down enough to think.

Yes, Edvard could be on the other side of the door. But he's not on duty tonight, or he wouldn't have been in the engine room. That means that there will be other men there who are on duty. I would even be happy to see Officer Garafolo when the hatch opens. I never thought that would happen.

I take a deep breath and shove. The hatch opens. I step over the coaming. It's not as dark as I thought it would be. The fog has lifted, and the wind has blown away any clouds so that the almost perfectly round moon is like a flashlight. I pull the door closed behind me and lean against it because my knees feel so wobbly.

Three men are on deck. Edvard isn't one of them.

They look at me, then turn away. They've never talked to me before or even smiled at me. Not like some of the others. To them, I'm the girl on board who brings bad luck, like gales and murdered wipers. Would they even listen to me? I can't take the time to find out.

I look up at the bridge. My father isn't there. First Mate Garafolo is looking down at something, maybe a chart. And next to him is Mrs. Dillon. If I climb up there and tell him what's happened, she would find out there's a murderer on board. She'd be frightened and tell the other passengers, and that would be it for my father's career as captain.

Oh, where is Papa? If he's not in his quarters and he's not on the bridge, where else could he be? And what do I do now? Go to my cabin and lock myself in? Wait for someone to look for me? But suppose that someone is not Papa or Danilo? Suppose that someone is Edvard?

Maybe my father is back in his quarters now. I'll have to go below deck again to find out. I can't let the passengers see me, not with grease and probably blood all over me. I've got to chance it. I say another prayer, to God and, this time, to my mother, too, and yank open the door I just came through, almost slide down the stairs and run toward my father's cabin.

God and Mom are listening. Papa's there and so is Danilo.

I stumble through the door, short of breath. Between that and my stammering, they both look like I'm speaking gibberish. Papa rises so quickly, his chair is knocked backwards.

"Francesca, what's happened? Where have you been? We've been looking all over the ship for you."

I'm still babbling. I'm grabbing a handful of the front of my blouse; I don't want it to touch my body. It has grease stains all over it. So do my legs and socks.

Papa rushes to me and touches my face very gently. I realize that it must be covered with blood. Then he wraps his hands around my upper arms and squats down—just a little because he's not that much taller than me—to look into my eyes.

"What is it? What's happened? Are you all right? Francesca, tell me! Who did this to you?"

Get a hold of yourself, Frances. Aunt Bess is back! Again, I listen to her. I look into Papa's eyes and speak, as calmly as possible.

"He knocked me out and tied me up and threw me into that awful place under the trap door."

Papa and Danilo both look confused, so I slow down even more.

"It's true. I'm not making it up. Edvard—you know, the deckhand who looks like Troy Donahue—he knocked me out and tied me up and blindfolded me and gagged me and threw me through the trap door in the engine room." I think that about covers everything.

Papa takes my hands in his and turns them over. Both he and Danilo catch their breath. I look at my hands for the first time since escaping the engine room. Besides the blood and scratches, there are nasty red marks on my wrists. Rope burns? My father slowly backs away and puts his hand on my throat. He walks in back of me and gently unknots the blindfold that's hanging from it. It falls to the floor. Then he yells, "Danilo!" as if Danilo were up on deck and not right in front of him.

I am safe. Papa and Danilo are here. So are the chief mate, the third mate, the second engineer. Papa is shouting at them. Every once in a while, I hear the name Troy. Finally, I realize that nobody understands who I'm talking about.

"Papa?" I try to get his attention, but my voice is hoarse and with all the noise, mainly coming from my father in both English and Italian, he doesn't hear me. I try again. "Papa!" I almost scream his name. Everybody goes quiet, and all the men look my way.

"Not Troy, Papa. Edvard." I can tell he still doesn't know who I'm talking about. I switch to Italian. "Edvard," I repeat. "He's one of the deck hands. Tall. He has blond hair. He's the one who did this to me." I can tell he knows who I'm talking about now. He shouts at the men in the cabin. But I'm feeling a little woozy, so all I catch is the name *Edvard* and the word *find*.

Now the cabin is empty of all the men except Drago, who is guarding me. He'll do a good job, I'm sure, but I walk to the door and lock it, just in case.

CHAPTER 61

Edvard

He is on his way back to the engine room to carry out his plan when he hears running footsteps and yelling. They're coming from overhead. The engineers' quarters are empty, so he slips in there and hides behind the door. It sounds like they finally realized the girl is missing and are searching for her. If one of the officers sees him, he might press him into helping them when what he most needs to do right now is shut the girl up for good.

The footsteps are closer now. Winston steps inside the cabin and stops, his head turning in one direction, then another. But he doesn't pull the door closed, so he doesn't see Edvard. Winston runs out.

Edvard hears him moving down the companionway and then stopping. Then he hears another voice, Nunziamo, the second mate.

"Did you check the engineers' quarters?"

"Yes, Sir."

"Carefully?"

Winston doesn't answer, not at first, and then, "I'd better check again, Sir. I might have missed something."

He did. He missed Edvard. Now he's found him.

"What are you doing here, hiding behind the door?"

Before Edvard can answer, Nunziamo enters.

"Sir, I found him hiding behind the door."

Nunziamo approaches Edvard, his chin jutting forward. Edvard is sure he could take on the second mate; he's not that big. But Winston is and looks like he's wishing Edvard would resist, so he could slug him. It's words Edvard needs now, not action.

"I wasn't hiding, Sir. I thought I saw a shadow, someone moving around in here." He assumes they're looking for the girl, but can't take

151

a chance that he's wrong by saying he thought the shadow might be her.

"And why is it your business if someone is in the engineers' quarters?"

There's only one logical answer to his question. Edvard has to chance that it's the right one.

"I thought it might be the girl, Sir."

"The girl? The captain's daughter?"

"Yes, Sir."

Winston and Nunziamo exchange a look that Edvard can't interpret, but before he can react, Winston yanks his arms behind his back as brutally as the bodyguard ever did.

Edvard now knows that someone must have found her and she told them about him. But how? How could they have found her?

They didn't, he finds out after he is taken to the captain's quarters. Somehow, she got away and told her father that Edvard tied her up and threw her into the hole underneath the trap door to die. Edvard should have killed her right away and would have if he'd known she was capable of escaping.

How did she escape, anyway? She couldn't yell, she couldn't see, and she couldn't move, not after he'd tied her up and blindfolded and gagged her. Yet, here she is.

Well, she's just another spoiled American brat, in Edvard's opinion. He knows how to handle this.

The captain's hands are balled into fists. He looks like he would like very much to use them on Edvard. Edvard needs to deflect that anger to the captain's daughter, so he assumes his innocent look—the one he perfected long before joining the *Ostvolk*—and addresses the captain.

"I don't know what she's talking about, Sir. Why would I hurt her?"

It looks like a question the captain wants answered, yet the fists haven't relaxed. He looks toward his daughter.

"Francesca?"

CHAPTER 62

Frankie

Why didn't I tell Papa what I thought when I first suspected Edvard? Why did I wait?

Because I thought he wouldn't be convinced unless I had proof. After my hiding in the warehouse in Baltimore and running away from Danilo in New Orleans, why should he? My behavior gave him every reason not to. So, I thought I needed proof, proof I didn't have. Saying that I saw Edvard in places he shouldn't have been and that he was probably on shore leave the same time as Kristian and that he's tall like the man I saw cutting open the mattresses—that wouldn't have been enough.

And it's not enough now. I still don't have that evidence. The blood and rope burns show that someone tied me up but not that it was Edvard. He's so convincing when he lies about it that I almost believe him myself. Well, at least I can answer the question he asked Papa.

"I know why he did this to me."

Papa looks at me and gives me his little encouraging smile, but only for a second before his eyes dart back to Edvard. "Why, *Cara*?"

"Because he knows I figured out that he killed the Wiper."

I thought Papa looked angry before, but now I'm scared he might kill Edvard before we find out the reason why he did it.

If I were Edvard, I'd be frightened of my father. Danilo has told me how strict he can be with, as Danilo describes them, "errant seamen." But Edvard doesn't look frightened. Instead, he is standing there looking like he feels sorry for me—and for Papa for having me for a daughter. I'd like to stomp on his foot or kick him where it hurts, anything to change that look on his face from pity to fear.

"Captain, I would never hurt your daughter. She's a girl. I would never hurt a girl." He looks like he means it, too, the liar. He hasn't fooled my father, though. Papa's hands are still curled into tight fists. But he also looks like he's trying to figure out why Edvard would murder Kristian.

And I can't answer that question.

I will not cry.

I will not cry because I am fifteen years old and able to defend myself against a lying, conceited murderer. Look at him standing there. He thinks he's going to get away with this. He thinks he's going to convince my father that I'm making it up or that I have an over-active imagination. Well, I'm not going to let him.

But suppose Papa does believe him? He probably knows Edvard as well as he knows me. Because, face it, Frankie, your father really doesn't know you at all. In your whole life, how much time has he spent with you? Two months a year times fifteen years? Thirty months in fifteen years? That's not a lot of time.

I want to run to my cabin and throw myself on the bunk and never come out. But then I look behind Papa at Danilo. Danilo smiles and nods. *Oh, Danilo, I am so sorry I ever thought you could have killed Kristian. I will never mistrust you again.*

I stand up straight. I will figure this out. I am a Moretti, after all.

"I've seen him all over the ship, Papa. In lots of places he wasn't supposed to be. The lounge and the galley and standing around the lifeboats like he was guarding them. And it must have been him I saw cutting open the mattresses in the engine room quarters." Why did it take me so long to realize this? "And tonight, I saw him come out of the engine room with something in his hand. He put it inside his sweater."

As I say this, I look at Edvard and, for just a second, he looks afraid. I turn back to my father. He's looking at Edvard, too. I'm sure he saw that look. At least I hope he did, because almost as soon as the fear appeared on his face, Edvard replaced it with that innocent look. How can he look that way when he's so guilty?

My father takes a step toward Edvard. "What was in his hand?" he asks me without taking his eyes off him.

"I don't know." He looks disappointed, so I rush on. "It looked like an envelope, like there was a letter inside, maybe." It wasn't much to go on, but my father must have thought otherwise.

"Danilo."

Danilo doesn't even ask Papa what he wants. He walks up to Edvard and orders him to put his arms over his head. Edvard does, but, honestly, anyone looking at him would think he was just some responsible citizen the police stopped by mistake. He's a much better actor than Troy Donahue.

Danilo frisks Edvard, front and back and sides, but finds nothing. Of course, Edvard wouldn't have it on him, whatever it is. He's too smart, for one thing, and he wouldn't look so—what's the word for it—cocky?

"Danilo, have two of the crew report to me. Then have Officer Nunziamo order the men to search his berth," Papa turns toward Edvard with a look that scares even me. "Look for an envelope or some papers. If they can't find it there, ask the second mate to have the crew search the rest of the ship." Danilo starts to leave.

"And Dani—"

"Yes, Sir."

"Have them look for anything else—anything—that might explain why he did this to Francesca."

On his way out the door, Danilo looks back and winks at me. That makes me feel good, but what makes me feel even better is that the snake, Edvard, has been caught.

CHAPTER 63

Edvard

He is still in the captain's quarters, with the captain, his daughter, and two of the deckhands. Guarding him? Protecting her? The captain has the radiator on full. Drops of sweat are running down Edvard's chest under his sweater. But not on his forehead, where the others could see it.

He's not nervous. The search is taking too long, and as far as he's concerned, that can only mean one thing. They can't find the document in his bunk or locker or anywhere on deck, so now they have to look elsewhere on the ship. They can look all night. They'll never locate it, and the captain's daughter will look like the fool she is.

Edvard clasps his hands behind his back and starts to roll back and forth on his feet. Then he notices the captain's glare and stops. He must be careful. The next minutes are crucial to convincing the captain that Edvard is innocent and that the girl is not well. He must look harmless, put-upon, wrongfully accused. If he can pull this off, not only will he be free to deliver the document when the ship arrives in Naples tomorrow, but the little brat will probably not be allowed out of her cabin for the rest of the voyage.

He assumes a new mask, the mask of the honorable, responsible mariner concerned for his superior officer and for that officer's troubled child.

CHAPTER 64

Frankie

Danilo walks in. He's not smiling.

"The men are still looking, Sir, but haven't found anything yet."

"They checked his bunk?"

Danilo nods. "And all the others. The mattresses in the engine room crew's quarters are ripped open at the seams, but there's nothing in them, Sir."

"His locker?"

Another nod.

"The lifeboats?

This time, Danilo's nod is short and annoyed. Of course, they checked all those places. That's what Papa ordered them to do.

"We've also checked the galley and the mess. The men are searching the saloon and lounge now. If they don't find it there or in the cargo holds, we'll have to check the passengers' cabins."

That would be a disaster, I know. It's late, and the passengers are probably all in bed. They won't like being disturbed. They won't like having their cabins searched like they were smugglers. And they definitely won't like knowing that they're sharing a ship with a murderer.

My father is looking down at the floor. He doesn't know what to do. I know this because he's running his hand through his hair like he does every time we discuss where I'm going to live. Then he tells Danilo and the two seamen to take Edvard to the bosun's store and post the two men outside the door.

This is not good. In fact, it's terrible. My father's in a tough spot. If he can't prove that Edvard is the killer and Edvard somehow convinces my father, or at least the other officers, that he wasn't the one who did this to me, then Papa will be in trouble with his bosses when we dock in Naples.

Once, he told Mom and me about another captain who arrested a seaman he thought was smuggling drugs. Only it turned it out that that seaman wasn't; another one was. That captain was demoted. That might happen to my father. Even worse, he might be fired, and it will all be my fault.

I can't seem to think; my mind is going around in circles. *Just take a breath and calm down*—there's Aunt Bess again. I will; then maybe I can figure out where it, whatever *it* is, is hidden.

Edvard is almost out the door when the chief mate walks in. In his hand are ropes and the handkerchief that Edvard stuffed into my mouth to gag me. There is blood on both.

"We found this under the trap door, Captain." Then he looks over at me, and for the first time since I met him, he's not frowning at me.

Now, my father's sitting on the edge of his desk, and I'm sitting in the chair he sits in to do his paperwork, correct my homework, and go over the navigational charts. He's holding both my hands and telling me over and over not to worry, to stay calm, to trust that the crew will find whatever it is that Edvard's hidden. This is all in Italian and sounds so sweet to me. I could listen all night long if I weren't doing just the opposite of what he says—worrying, being antsy, and fearing that the crew will not find whatever it is that Edvard hid.

Danilo is back. The men have found nothing yet, and they've been looking a long time. None of us are looking at each other. We're all looking at the floor.

I'm the first one to speak.

"I'm sorry, Papa." What I'm sorry about is that I lied to him, that I didn't tell him of my suspicions, that I have no evidence, and that he is being put in such a terrible situation. But I don't know how to say all that, so I just repeat, "I'm sorry."

He smiles and says "*Va bene, Tesoro.*" But it's not all right. Everything's a mess, and it's all my fault. No, not all. I didn't murder Kristian. I didn't knock myself out and tie myself up and throw myself into that hole under the engine room floor.

Maybe they'll have to let him go if they can't prove he did this to me, if he convinces them that I have him mixed up with another crew member. Will he try to hurt me again? Kill me? He wouldn't dare. He must know what Papa would do if he did.

The worst part is that they will have to wake up the passengers and search their cabins. At least one of them will complain to the Home Office, and my father will get into trouble, maybe even get fired. Either way, I'm pretty sure I'll be off the ship.

I close my eyes to see if that helps me think. I remember Edvard always smiling at me. I remember him giving me candy. I remember thinking that he liked me and wish I could unremember it, it's so embarrassing. I remember walking past him on deck and in the companionways and—

My eyes pop open. I remember another time I saw him, and it was not on the deck or by the lifeboats or in the lounge. Why was he there? I wondered at the time. He's not a cook; he's not a steward. When he saw me, he looked annoyed. I was hurt because I thought it meant he didn't like me anymore.

"Papa!"

"What is it, Francesca?"

"I think I know where he hid it." And then I turn and run out the door.

CHAPTER 65

Edvard

He keeps flexing his fists, ready to strike at his enemy. He wants to wrap his hands around the skinny little neck of that brat and squeeze and squeeze until there's no life left. Why didn't he kill her right away? He had the document by then. He only had to hide it and play the innocent when he was asked if he'd seen the captain's missing daughter. He would have dodged any blame, just as he always has.

But it's not over yet. They won't find the document; therefore, they won't find a reason for Edvard to harm the kid. And then he'll be able to convince her father that she has him mixed up with another sailor, that what happened to her was so traumatic that it's affected her memory. When the captain ordered the crew to keep searching the ship, Edvard could see the doubt on their faces. That doubt will become a certainty when they don't find anything. Then he will be released, and it will be the girl who's ordered to stay in her cabin.

And when it reaches Naples, *Il Destino's* owners will kick her, and probably her father, off the ship.

And Edvard will follow them. He will be taking shore leave, a permanent one, from being a deck hand and from pretending to be a genial shipmate. He will have his $5000 and the document, and he will be on his way home.

He looks forward to seeing the expression on the bodyguard's face when he hands the document to him and to the Leader's gratitude for Edvard's success.

CHAPTER 66

Frankie

My father and Danilo are behind me, shouting for me to stop, but I don't. Not until I reach the freezer.

This is where I saw Edvard. I was hurt when he didn't smile at me like he usually did. Now, I know all those smiles were fake, that he was just being nice to me because he wanted to stay on the good side of the captain's daughter. I feel my face getting red. I don't think it's because I've been running.

When I reach the door of the freezer, I don't stop to catch my breath. I can do that later. I grab the handle and yank. The door is heavy, but I tug it open all the way, so hard that it crashes against the wall beside it.

My father and Danilo are next to me now. They're out of breath, too.

"It's in here. I know it is."

"Francesca—."

"Please, Papa. I know what I'm doing. It's here. I saw him once. He was just coming out of here, and I remember wondering what he could have been doing."

My father nods at me, then walks into the freezer with Danilo and me right behind him.

It's cold, and even though it's huge, crowded. There are cardboard boxes stacked against every wall and skinned animals hanging from hooks. I don't look at them too closely, so I'm not sure what they are. Cows? Pigs? The boxes are white and taped shut. Will we have to untape and search every one?

My father climbs up to the highest boxes to check if anything is on top of them. He shakes his head and then pushes his hand down between the wall and the top box nearest him. Danilo runs his hand down the space behind the boxes stacked at the end of the right wall while I run mine behind the boxes stacked at the end of the left wall.

Danilo lifts down the first box and puts it on the floor of the freezer. My father climbs down, kneels, opens it and takes out what's inside— bags of green beans—but finds nothing else. He throws the bags back into the box and opens the next one Danilo's placed on the floor. This one has shrimp in it, not in bags, just loose. My father thrusts his hands into the box and moves them around, lifting shrimp from the bottom, running his hands around the sides, causing some of the shrimp to fall on the freezer floor. Then, he shakes his head. Nothing there.

The freezer is too small for the three of us to move around in. We keep bumping into and snapping at each other.

"This isn't going to work," he mumbles. "Francesca, there's not enough room in here. You go outside."

I walk out of the freezer, lean against the wall opposite and watch as Danilo takes down box after box and my father searches each one. All I can think about is how long it will take them to open every box and pull out all the food to look for whatever was in Edvard's hand. Even with three of us looking, we could be here a long time.

As I lean against the wall, I scan the boxes that Danilo hasn't touched yet. If it was an envelope I saw Edvard put under his sweater, he would have to make sure that the writing on whatever was inside it didn't get damaged by moisture. That would be hard to do with frozen stuff. He'd be really taking a chance if he put it inside any of the boxes.

Edvard would realize that. Does that mean he didn't hide it in the freezer, after all?

No! He could still hide it there. But not *inside* one of the boxes. Outside it.

"Papa!"

My father pulls his red, wet hands out of the seventh box he's opened and looks up at me, his eyebrows raised.

"Underneath, Papa." I look up at Danilo, who's holding the eighth box in his hands, which are almost as red as Papa's. "Edvard taped it underneath one of the boxes. I'm sure of it."

Danilo looks under the box he's holding and shakes his head no. He turns and starts lifting the other boxes off the stack, raising each over his head and checking the underside. Meanwhile, Papa is doing the same to the boxes he's already searched, picking each one up and looking at the bottom.

Nothing. They're finding nothing. They both look at me as if I would know which ones they should look under. And I do.

"Look at the boxes on the bottom of the stacks."

It seems so obvious now. Edvard wouldn't tape it to a box that would be opened soon. One of the cooks would find it. Instead, he'd put it underneath a box that would probably not be opened until we left Naples. We would be at sea, and Edvard would be on shore with whatever he'd hidden under the box.

Danilo hands my father box after box until he reaches the bottom level of each stack. Both of them turn to me as if waiting for my orders. I nod and they start upending each of the ones on the bottom layer.

And there they find it. Taped to the underside of the fourth box is an envelope. A dirty, gray envelope, torn at the bottom corner, with writing too smudged to read on the front.

CHAPTER 67

Frankie

We are back in my father's quarters, cramped, because in addition to Papa, Danilo, and me, the chief mate and Drago are there. My father has opened the envelope we found and pulled out two letter-sized pieces of paper and another piece, half their size, thin and flimsy, almost see-through. Its ink has rubbed off on Papa's fingers. He places it aside and lays the other two sheets on his desk. He leans over, his hands on either side of them. We all look over his shoulder.

The chief mate snorts. Drago's shoulders slump. Danilo looks at me as if I might know the answer to the puzzle, but I don't.

The puzzle is, what does it say? And what language does it say it in? It's not English or Italian. We all know that it's not French or Spanish. Danilo assures my father that it's not any Filipino language he's ever seen, and Drago assures him that it isn't Croatian or Serbian or Greek.

"German? Could it be German?" As soon as I ask it, I know the answer. Edvard said he was from West Germany, but that was probably a lie. Before I can say this, Officer Garafolo says, "Not German." He learned that language during the war.

"We'll have to wait until we reach Naples tomorrow and have the police figure this out." Drago and Danilo nod in agreement with the first mate's suggestion.

"No," my father says. "We can figure this out now." That's my Papa all over—he never lets up until he solves a problem.

"How do you plan to do that, Sir?"

Silence. No one has an answer to Drago's question. Except me.

"I know how. We'll use the information on the list." I don't need to check it. I can remember every name, every nationality on it.

"What list?" Drago places his hand on my shoulder.

164

"A list of all the seamen on *Il Destino* and when they signed up and where they came from. Kristian was from Estonia, so maybe it's Estonian." Now my secret is out, but no one questions how I got this information.

"Kristian." I look from face to face, but it's obvious that they've all forgotten, even my father, what I told them earlier about who Edvard murdered. I feel like a school teacher whose students can't grasp long division. "Kristian Sisask," I pronounce each syllable. "The Wiper. The dead Wiper."

CHAPTER 68

Frankie

My father's small office is even more cramped now. Kaarel Harma, the only Estonian on board, is there, studying the two pages spread out on the table. He's been doing that so long I think he must be memorizing the words. His teeth are biting down on his lower lip, but he's not making any other moves. He's not shaking or nodding his head. He's not smiling or frowning. His hands are behind his back, and they're not moving either. Only his eyes are, from one sheet of paper to the other and then to the carbon paper, which looks like it might be a copy of a check, according to Officer Garafolo, or a copy of a receipt, according to Drago.

Besides the sound of the waves outside the porthole, my father's foot tapping, and the chief mate's breath wheezing, the room is quiet, like we're in a library. Danilo's shoulders are hunched, and his hands are pressed against his mouth. Drago has his hands hanging at his sides, the fingers of both soundlessly drumming against his pants legs. We are all staring at the Estonian. Am I the only one who wants to shout at him to hurry up?

Finally, he looks up at Papa.

"This is not in my language," he announces.

It's like something has sucked the air from the room. Drago hits his thighs with his fists, and the chief mate looks heavenward. Papa runs his hand through his hair. Both the officers mutter something. They're probably cursing, but don't do it out loud because of me. Only Danilo doesn't move or speak, his eyes still on the Estonian, like he's waiting for something to happen.

Then it does.

Kaarel Harma looks at us all. "It's not Estonian," he repeats. "But I know what it is. I know this language."

And because Kaarel Harma knows the language, we now understand why Kristian Sisask died.

CHAPTER 69

Edvard

He is glad to step into the early morning Italian sunlight even if his hands are cuffed behind his back and he is surrounded by four policemen. They are taking him to an Italian prison, but at least he will no longer be on water. He will be on land—solid land. Land won't be constantly pitching back and forth and swaying from side to side. He'll be able to walk steadily from place to place, even if the places are just a prison cell and a prison yard.

He failed in his mission. The captain's daughter saw to that. A girl who had no idea what was at stake if the document fell into the wrong hands is responsible for it doing just that. The Neapolitan police will look at it and decide who sees it next—probably their government or maybe the rebels in Edvard's country.

And that will be the end of the Leader and of his dream and Edvard's own, the dream of restoring their country to its former greatness. When the Leader loses power, will the Italians send Edvard back to his country to serve his sentence? The Leader will no longer be in power, and those who are will see his actions as treason, punishable by death. A firing squad? A noose? Well, at least, he will die where he was born.

Or maybe not. Maybe he won't live that long. As he steps onto the gangway to disembark, he looks down and sees the bodyguard.

CHAPTER 70

Frankie

We will be at sea again when the government that Edvard killed for falls. It will take a few weeks, the Neapolitan prosecutor says, for the news of their leader's treachery to reach the citizens of his country through the underground network of freedom fighters. My father says the copy of the check alone might topple him. Five million dollars is a lot of money for one man, especially in a country so poor. In Kristian's country, it would buy many homes, a yacht, and lots of jewelry. In Italy, Papa says, more than a thousand people could live well for a year on that money.

But it is where the money came from that will bring an end to the dictator's rule of Edvard and Kristian's homeland. It came from a Hungarian politician in payment for the rights to mine the shale in the dictator's country. I'd never heard of shale before, but Papa says that you can get uranium from it, and uranium is one of the things you need to make an atomic bomb. The fact that the dictator would sell his country's precious resource alone will ensure his fall from power and probably his death. The Wiper, Kristian Sisask, risked his life and eventually lost it to bring the document to the attention of his countrymen. Maybe they will build a statue in his honor.

There Edvard is, hands in handcuffs behind his back, an Italian policeman in front of him, one in back, and one on each side. He won't be getting away this time. I don't know where he'll end up. Maybe in Baltimore because that's where he killed Kristian. Maybe in an Italian jail. Maybe back in the country he came from. Well, as Aunt Bess would say, *Good riddance to bad rubbish.*

I finally finished my letter to Tricia. It took a long time because it's a long letter. I wrote everything that's happened to me since I boarded *Il*

Destino in Baltimore—the warehouse, the chase through New Orleans, being tied up in the space underneath the trap door, and Edvard's capture. I even wrote about my stupidity in thinking Edvard might like me. I'll mail it as soon as I go ashore.

I'm so happy that I was able to find out who murdered Kristian, but angry at myself because my first plan to catch him didn't work—the plan where I would figure out which crew members came from the same country and might have known each other in the past.

My Miss Marple idea would have worked if they'd told the truth. It's obvious to me why Edvard lied and said he was from West Germany. But why did Kristian lie? Because he was running away from his enemies? Hiding until he could get the document back to his fellow freedom fighters? Whatever the reason, Kristian was a hero, and sometimes it's okay for heroes to lie.

But was it okay for me to lie? I lied to so many people—Papa, Danilo, Officer Garafolo. I felt it was for a good reason, but now I'm not so sure. Well, it won't happen again. I promise I will never lie to Papa or Danilo again. I'm not so sure about the chief mate, though.

Well, it's all over. Now, I can stand here at the bow early in the morning and not worry about catching a killer. I feel like I could stand here forever.

I love being on the ocean. The stars in the night sky, so many it seemed that there was barely space between them, when we were finally out at sea and out of sight of land. It scared me then, all that sky, all that water. Suppose the ship goes down, I remember thinking. I'm not that good of a swimmer. And even if I could swim far enough to find land, I wouldn't know which direction to go.

When I was little, I used to complain to Mom that Papa was away too much and why couldn't he be like my friends' fathers who came home every night for dinner. She would laugh and say, "One day, Frankie, when you're a little older and know your Papa a little better, you'll understand." Well, I'm older now, and I know what she meant, why Papa loves it so much. I think it makes him feel free. I know it makes me feel free.

And there's so much to see once a ship loses sight of land. Sometimes I don't know which way to look. Up at the sun, the moon, the shooting stars. At the little black and white birds that fly so far from land that it's a wonder that they don't get tired and drop into the ocean. Or down and be lucky enough to catch sight of a school of dolphins jumping in our wake. Or up *and* down to watch the flying fish soaring up out of the water at night and gliding through the air like planes.

I want to live here on *Il Destino*, even though Papa was right before and I was wrong. It was dangerous for me to be on a ship when there might have been a killer on board.

But it's not dangerous any more. The killer is gone, the ship is safe, and there's no reason why *Il Destino* can't be my home.

Acknowledgements

It is one thing to begin a novel and another to finish it. What has sustained me in this effort has been the Writers Center in Bethesda, Maryland, and my novel writing group. The many courses available at the Center were so helpful to me in the completion of this book. I especially want to thank Kathryn Johnson, whose Extreme Novelist seminar once again kept me going until I completed my first draft of *Captain Moretti's Daughter*.

Also, through the Writers Center, I met my writers group—Rose Ann Cleveland, Julie Corrigan, Jennifer Hale, Maria Karametou, and Elizbeth Smiroldo. As with my first novel, *Once Upon a Time in Baltimore*, these women gave me much valuable advice and support. I was fortunate to have found them.

Since I did not know much about what an Italian Merchant Marine freighter operating in 1960 was like, I took a trip on the John W. Brown (https://www.ssjohnwbrown.org/), which offers tours and short cruises out of the port of Baltimore. Its knowledgeable volunteer crew, especially Captain Mike Smith, patiently answered my many questions. Of course, any "nautical" errors in the book are solely mine.

Finally, a special thanks to my husband, Joe, and my son, Michael, for their sustained support and encouragement.

www.ingramcontent.com/pod-product-compliance
Lightning Source LLC
Chambersburg PA
CBHW070910030726
47504CB00005B/1535